THE DOCKLAND ORPHAN

LILY BOURNE

CHAPTER 1

Nell Warrington stood at the edge of the Limehouse docks, watching as the early morning sun pierced the fog that lay across the Thames. The river gleamed in patches where the mist had begun to shred, and she drew in a deep breath, the sharp scent of fish prickling her nostrils. She let the cold air clear her head, grateful for this moment of solitude before the day's inevitable confrontations began.

The *Elizabeth*, flagship of the Warrington Shipping Company and named for her late mother, was moored beside the quay, her crew busy unloading the latest consignment from Calcutta. Nell surveyed the scene with quiet authority. Her father would have cut an imposing figure on these docks; she hoped she might do the same, despite her more diminutive stature.

The foreman approached, cap clutched in his hands, his forced cheerfulness doing little to conceal his distaste for a woman at the helm of such an enterprise.

"That's the lot, Miss Warrington," he said, gesturing broadly toward the stacked goods. "All unloaded, present and correct."

She gave him a cursory smile, her gaze drifting methodically over the crates stacked upon the dock. Consulting the docket in her hand, her brow furrowed.

"Is it?" she replied coolly. "Seems to me there's a crate missing. Number forty-seven."

The foreman glanced uneasily towards a cluster of dockworkers loitering nearby, rolling his eyes in silent appeal. A couple of the men sniggered.

"Don't believe so, Miss," he said, though his voice lacked conviction. "Perhaps there's been some confusion with the manifest."

Without another word, Nell gathered her skirts and strode up the gangplank and into the dim recesses of the cargo hold. In one shadowy corner, half-hidden beneath a tarpaulin, she found the missing crate. She called the foreman aboard and pointed directly at it.

"Seems you're having trouble with your arithmetic this morning, Mr. Foreman" she said. "Get that unloaded so I can sign the paperwork and you can be about your business."

She turned on her heel and descended the gangplank, her skirts swishing behind her. The murmurs behind her swelled as she passed through the docks, the men's voices ripe with muttering and mockery.

But her composure did not falter. She had weathered far worse in the nine months since her father had left for India on business. The whispers in drawing rooms were often crueller than anything these rough men could devise.

Only once she reached the shipping office allowed herself a moment's pause. The clock on the wall chimed eight; an early start, but necessary if she were to keep on top of things.

She gathered up the ledgers, tucked them under her arm, and made her way upstairs to her father's office—a room she had largely left untouched since his hasty departure for India. The door creaked open, revealing the masculine sanctuary with its leather-bound books and lingering scent of pipe tobacco. Though she had added her own modest touches: a small vase of flowers, a more comfortable chair, it remained emphatically his domain.

As did the business itself, at least in the eyes of society. But until his return, she would ensure that Warrington Shipping prospered.

She sat down heavily in the chair and placed the pile of ledgers on the desk, accidentally knocking over a framed photograph as she did so. She picked it up with care, her fingers tracing the faces within the frame. Her father looked remarkably younger then, more carefree, with his arm proudly encircling her mother's waist. He had often remarked on how much Nell resembled her, and the likeness was striking: the same rich chestnut hair, the same slight stature, and that same proud tilt of the chin that made her appear ten feet tall despite her size.

She had often wondered why her father looked so different now. For years, she hadn't been able to put her finger on it. But now she understood with painful clarity. It was the absence of light in his eyes, the sadness that had taken up permanent residence there. Guilt tugged at her once again. Her mother had died bringing her into the world, and though he had never spoken of it directly, it was clear that day had broken him. Nell had spent much of her life trying to convince him that the sacrifice had been worth it.

With a sigh, she shook herself from the memory and returned to the present, rifling through the morning post. Another letter from a creditor, payment overdue by two weeks. It had been these mounting debts that had driven her father to accept the temporary assignment with the East India Company, just nine months prior. A principled man, he had loathed the Company, believing it corrupt and self-serving. But he had taken the post regardless, in the hope it would finally clear the family's considerable debts.

Now, Nell found herself wondering what that sacrifice would truly cost him.

She rested her head in her hands, the weight of her father's legacy pressing down on her. *Don't fail him now*, she thought. *Don't lose everything he worked for.*

She had just begun poring over the ledgers again, searching desperately for some way out of their predicament, when a sharp knock at the door disturbed her thoughts. Before she had time to respond, the door swung open.

A tall man stepped into the room, his presence commanding. Broad-shouldered and marked with a jagged scar across the cheek, he exuded menace. Startled by the intrusion, Nell rose swiftly from her chair.

"Can I help you? This is a private office. The shipping office is downstairs."

He strode further into the room. "I know exactly where I am. Miss Warrington, isn't it?"

She faltered slightly, but straightened her back and lifted her chin. "Then I'll ask again, Sir. How can I help you?"

He gave a low, humourless laugh. "Don't often get called 'Sir' in my line of work, miss."

"Really?" she said evenly. "And what line of work would that be?"

"I represent a company your father knows very well," he said, taking another step toward her. There was a glint in his eye that set her nerves alight. "A company he owes a considerable sum to."

Nell's cheeks flushed. She reached for her quill. "Then I'm quite certain we can come to some suitable arrangement with your employers, Mr—?"

"I'm afraid it's a little too late for that," he said coldly, not offering his name.

"Come now," she said, striving to keep her tone calm. "I'm certain we can reach an agreement that would satisfy all parties concerned—"

But before she could finish, he was across the room with alarming swiftness. In a flash, he was behind the desk, grabbing her by the throat and slamming her against the wall.

"Oh no, miss," he sneered. "Don't try your feminine wiles on me."

Struggling for breath beneath his crushing grip, Nell managed to gasp, "Sir... you misunderstand. I meant a financial arrangement."

"Your father already defaulted on his last financial arrangement," he growled. "Luckily for you, I'm here to give one final warning. Repayments must be brought up to date by month's end. Otherwise, I'll return, and I won't be so polite next time."

As he loosened his grip and she drew a painful breath of air, he struck her, twice, with brutal efficiency in the ribs. The wind was knocked from her lungs, and she collapsed to the floor, coughing violently.

She remained there, curled behind the desk, one hand clutching her bruised side, until she heard the office door slam and his heavy footsteps descending the stairs. Only then did she permit herself a single, choked sob.

Through the window, she could hear the ordinary sounds of the docks continuing. Men shouting, cargo being moved, the distant whistle of a steam packet.

Like the others on the docks, Nell knew she had to carry on as though nothing had happened. Business as usual. She forced herself upright, brushing down her clothes and inspecting the damage. A large, angry bruise was already blooming across her ribs, and several cuts marked her side where the man's heavy rings had gouged into her skin. Blood had trickled down and soaked into her blouse.

Leaning over her desk, she steadied herself, forcing her mind to work despite the pain. She considered visiting the family doctor, elderly Dr Fitzgerald, who would no doubt treat her with care. But she couldn't trust that he'd keep such injuries from her father. Not entirely. She remembered how, some time ago, a group of dockworkers had been involved in a fight they'd wanted to keep quiet, and one of them had sought treatment in the Chinese quarter. The apothecaries there had a reputation for discretion.

She snatched one of her father's scarves from the coat stand and wrapped it around her ribs, wincing with every movement. Then she shrugged on his greatcoat, hoping it would conceal the blood staining her bodice. Taking a deep breath, she composed herself and walked out of the office, her steps slightly uneven.

A dockhand approached hastily, lifting a crate in one arm.

"Miss Warrington, there's something needs your attention if you've got a minute?"

"I'm sorry," she said through gritted teeth. "I'm being called away on urgent business. I'll return shortly."

She ignored his muttered response, certain he'd hurry back to the others with more fodder for the ever-growing mound of rumours. But she couldn't concern herself with that now. Moving as quickly as she could manage, she made her way through the winding streets of London, heading towards the Chinese quarter.

The narrow street there was a maze of herbal smells and coloured lanterns, lined with small apothecaries, each window filled with glass jars, dried roots, and folded paper packets. She passed them slowly, peering into each, looking for someone who might offer both skill and silence.

Near the end of the street, she stopped. This last shop had a woman behind the counter—the only one run by a woman she'd seen. Intrigued, Nell limped to the door and pushed it open, a little bell tinkling softly above.

The woman behind the counter looked up from her bottles, raising a single eyebrow. The rest of her face remained neutral. She was short and fine-boned, likely around Nell's age, with glossy black hair plaited neatly down her back. As Nell wandered between the shelves, feigning interest, she watched the woman move, quiet, methodical, efficient. It seemed she hadn't taken much notice of Nell, until Nell took a step forward and cried out as pain shot through her leg and up into her ribs.

She collapsed to the floor, gasping.

The woman was beside her in a heartbeat, sliding an arm beneath her elbow to help her up.

"Are you well, miss? May I assist you?"

"I'm quite all right," Nell said, regaining her composure.

"Are you sure?" the woman asked, glancing meaningfully at the floor where a small pool of blood had begun to form.

They exchanged a knowing look. Without another word, the woman guided her through the shop and into a small back room.

"Please, sit. We won't be disturbed here. My name is Mei Ling."

Nell hesitated.

"Don't worry," said Mei Ling softly. "I don't need to know yours."

Mei Ling said nothing further, merely took Nell's coat and gently unwrapped the scarf from around her ribs. With quiet competence, she began cleaning the wounds, dabbing tinctures along the cuts and bruises that now spread like a storm cloud across her side.

When she finished, she stepped back. "I think you'll be all right. Let me get you something to take home."

She disappeared into the Mein shop, then returned moments later with a packet of mixed powders.

"Do you work at the docks?" she asked casually.

Nell's head shot up, alarmed.

"Don't worry," Mei Ling said with a gentle smile. "I don't know you. But I can smell the river on your coat. And that—" she nodded toward Nell's bruised side "—looks like the work of someone with heavy hands."

Nell looked down at the floor, saying nothing.

Mei Ling held out the packet. "Mix this with water and apply it to the wounds every few days."

As Nell took it, the apothecary added in a quieter

voice, "There are ways and means to stay afloat, you know. If one knows who to speak to."

She smiled calmly and said no more.

As Nell left the shop, she felt strangely unsettled, but also comforted. It was as if Mei Ling had seen something in her that others did not. That awareness lingered with her, though she could not explain it.

Back at the docks, she stood by the office window, staring out over the Thames, her coat pulled tightly around her aching ribs.

"Don't worry, Papa," she whispered. "I'll find another way. I won't compromise your principles."

CHAPTER 2

The docks buzzed with life as the courier made his way through the crowd of dockhands busy at their work. He wove carefully between them, dodging swinging cargo nets and taking care not to trip over coiled ropes strewn across the uneven cobblestones.

Rumours had reached him about the letter he carried. Whispers passed in hushed tones over wooden crates and foaming pints of bitter. He was keenly aware of several pairs of eyes following his progress as he strode purposefully towards the Warrington Shipping Office. If the stories were true, it wouldn't be Miss Warrington who paid the price, not really. It would be the families of the sailors. It always was. The girl and her stiff-backed father would carry on. The rest would suffer.

He knocked on the door of the office and stepped inside. The front counter stood unattended, but he detected footsteps descending from the floor above, accompanied by a barely audible intake of breath with each step.

"I shall be down in just a moment," came a strained voice from above.

A moment later, Nell appeared at the top of the stairs, carefully lifting the hem of her skirts while pressing one elbow discreetly against her side. Her movements were measured, her breath tight. As she reached the final step, she placed her right foot gingerly on the floor, as though testing its strength.

"Good morning," she said, her tone admirably composed despite the obvious discomfort she was in. "Is it the mail?"

The young man nodded, rummaging through his satchel. "Yes, miss. Special delivery from the harbour master's office. I was told to bring it with all possible haste."

A flicker of unease passed over Nell's face. *What now?* she thought.

She picked the envelope from the counter but

paused as she noticed the courier still standing there, watching her with open curiosity.

"Thank you," she said crisply. "That will be all."

He hesitated, clearly reluctant to depart without witnessing her reaction, but then backed out of the office with obvious disappointment. As he opened the door, Nell glimpsed a small crowd gathering just outside. Their heads turned as one, pretending not to look even as they strained to catch sight of her.

I'll deal with that later, she thought, closing the door behind him.

She pulled open a drawer of the polished counter, extracted her father's old ivory paper knife, and carefully slit the envelope along its edge Inside was a folded parchment, standard correspondence, but her hands trembled as she unfolded it.

Miss Warrington,

It is with profound regret that we must inform you that the Warrington Shipping Company vessel the 'Eleanor' has been lost at sea.

Last known contact was recorded just prior to her passing the Cape of Good Hope, some fortnight ago.

We must report, with the gravest sorrow, that there appear to be no survivors of this tragic event. Two damaged crates were retrieved from wreckage discovered near the coastline, contents largely unsalvageable.

I remain, with sincere condolences,

Your obedient servant, Edward Wilberforce Local Shipping Master Cape of Good Hope

Nell sank to the floor, the wind expelled from her chest in a manner now distressingly familiar. The sensation mirrored precisely the moment the debt collector's fist had driven into her ribs. Only this blow felt deeper, colder, and infinitely more devastating.

This cannot be happening. Not now. Not after everything else.

The *'Eleanor'* was gone. That meant the company's once-proud fleet had been reduced to merely three vessels, and with it, any hope of meeting their mounting financial obligations had grown even more remote.

Through a veil of unshed tears, Nell stared at the letter, willing the words to rearrange themselves into some message less catastrophic. But the black ink remained cruelly so, bearing witness to yet another crushing blow to the Warrington name.

Once again, Nell picked herself up from the floor, drawing herself to her full height despite the persistent ache in her side. Now she understood with grim certainty what the expectant crowd outside the office door had gathered for.

Dabbing her eyes with the edge of her handkerchief, she took a steadying breath and opened the door to a sea of expectant faces. The foreman stepped forward.

"Is it true, Miss Warrington?" he asked, his voice uncharacteristically gentle.

She surveyed the assembled throng, her heart rising into her throat as she recognised the faces of several wives, now widows, of the crew lost at sea. Mrs. Barton with her three small children clinging to her skirts; old Mrs. Hayward, whose son had been the ship's carpenter; young Emily Fletcher, barely eighteen and married only a fortnight before the *Eleanor* had set sail.

"I'm afraid it's true," she said, her voice steadier than she felt. "We've had some very bad news. A report has come in from the local shipping master at the Cape of Good Hope. Parts of the wreckage of the *Eleanor* have been recovered."

She looked up, meeting their eyes with quiet resolve.

"I regret to inform you that there are, as yet, no survivors."

A cry went up, raw and gut-wrenching. Two of the women clutched each other, sobbing uncontrollably whilst a third sank to her knees upon the rough cobblestones. A heavy silence settled over the men, their faces grave and ashen.

"I am so very sorry to deliver this dreadful news," Nell continued, fighting to maintain her composure. "Of course, the company will do everything within its power to support the bereaved families."

The foreman, glancing uneasily at some of the other dockworkers, added, "Best get onto that insurance company right quick, Miss. These families will need a way to get by, what with winter coming on and all."

Nell turned to him, her face composed though her insides twisted with dread. *Please let that be one debt Father cleared,* she thought.

"Yes, of course," she said quickly. "Please excuse me, I shall make the necessary arrangements immediately. I'll be in touch with each family shortly. In the meantime, as a mark of respect, the company will close operations for the day."

A low murmur rippled through the crowd.

"Paid, of course," she added, hoping once again that she wasn't making promises she couldn't possibly honour.

The foreman muttered to a colleague, just loud enough for her to hear, "Be a blessed sight nicer to get paid for last week's labour first…"

Nell turned to him sharply. "Everything is under control, Mr Larkin. Please don't worry."

Though nothing, in truth, could be further from reality.

As the sombre crowd dispersed, she shut the door behind her and leaned heavily against it, catching her breath as pain flared through her bruised ribs. Gathering her resolve, she made her way up the stairs as swiftly as her injuries would permit and sank into her father's chair,

Where would he have kept the insurance documents? she wondered, scanning the office shelves where he typically stored correspondence of importance. But the familiar mahogany boxes yielded nothing.

Then her eyes caught on a small brass key lying in a shallow tray on his desk. She picked it up, turning it over between her fingers. Pushing the chair back, she crouched beside the desk, wincing at the discomfort, and methodically examined each drawer.

None had ever been locked. Until now.

She spotted a narrow panel at the bottom, almost invisible unless one knew to look for it. Trying the key, she felt the mechanism turn with a satisfying click. A hidden compartment sprang open.

Inside was a thin stack of folded documents. She

removed them with trembling hands and placed them on the desk, beginning to rifle through them, hoping desperately for relief, yet dreading what she might discover.

Her heart sank with each passing second.

They were letters from creditors. Dozens of them. Shipping authorities, accountants, landlords, each parchment stamped in red ink. *Defaulted. Overdue. Final notice.*

The despair rose in her throat like bile. The situation was far worse than she'd imagined.

Then came the worst revelation of all: a cluster of letters from Cohen & Cohen Maritime Insurers. Five or six increasingly firm demands for overdue payments, culminating in a final notice: the policy had been voided. Her father had defaulted on the premiums for over six months. The *Eleanor*, and the men who sailed her, had not been insured when disaster struck.

No... she thought, the breath leaving her body.

Her father had always cared deeply for his people. How could he have allowed this catastrophe to happen? More than twenty families now stood to lose everything. Not only their beloved husbands, fathers and sons, but any financial protection that might have kept them from the workhouse

The culmination of weeks of pressure, loss, and fear broke over her like a tidal wave. She collapsed over the desk, sobbing uncontrollably, unable to see any way out.

How can I possibly make this right? she thought despairingly. We shall lose the company... our family's reputation... and they will all despise us for it. Justifiably so.

She didn't know how long she lay there, but when she lifted her head and wiped her tears away, the moonlight had already spilled across the office floor. She'd been asleep, fitfully, curled in grief.

Then she froze.

Footsteps.

Almost imperceptible. Someone was ascending the stairs with deliberate stealth.

She pushed the chair back silently, her heartbeat hammering in her ears. Moving quickly despite her injuries, she grasped one of her father's sturdy umbrellas from the coat stand. Rising from her seat as noiselessly as possible, she crossed the room and pressed herself against the wall beside the door, the umbrella raised above her head ready to strike.

The footsteps drew closer. The brass handle turned with agonizing slowness.

A scent wafted toward her, faint but curiously

familiar. Herbal. Calming. She couldn't quite place it, though it stirred some distant memory.

As the door opened, she raised the umbrella high, bracing herself for the appearance of a looming, menacing figure.

But the person who stepped through was considerably smaller than she had anticipated. In the pale moonlight, Nell observed the distinctive glint of a long, glossy black plait falling elegantly down the visitor's back.

She let out an audible sigh of relief, the umbrella wavering in her grasp.

Mei Ling stepped inside, turning just in time to see the umbrella mid-air, and Nell's face, pale and wild with tension.

"Oh, my," Mei Ling exclaimed, raising a small fist reflexively in a defensive posture. But the sight of Nell, battle-ready with such an incongruous weapon, was simply too much. She dissolved into peals of laughter that echoed in the moonlit office.

"I see that despite your injuries, you remain formidable, Miss Warrington," she said, her English perfect but with the faintest trace of an accent. "Though I daresay an umbrella would prove rather ineffectual against a genuine assailant."

Relief flooded through her, and Nell burst into

laughter, the first time she had done so in months, she realised. The sound seemed almost foreign to her ears. Setting the umbrella back into the coat stand, she returned to her seat behind the desk, wincing slightly as she sat.

"Please, take a seat," she said to Mei Ling. "What brings you here at this hour?"

Mei Ling smiled and reached into her silk bag, producing several small packets of herbs and powders.

"I thought you might be in need of more of these, for your wounds," she said gently. "I didn't want to come during the day and arouse suspicion."

"Thank you," Nell said warmly. "That's very kind of you."

Mei Ling placed the packets on the desk and regarded Nell thoughtfully, her dark, perceptive eyes missing nothing of Nell's dishevelled appearance and the telltale redness around her eyes.

"I hope you don't think I'm prying," she began, selecting her words carefully, "but... is everything quite all right?"

Reflexively, Nell answered, "Why, yes, of course. Merely the usual business concerns, I'm sure you know how it is"

A silence stretched between them, filled with the quiet hum of night outside the window.

"I hope you know," Mei Ling said softly, "that you can be assured of my discretion. And… as I'm only too aware myself, women who must survive in a man's world can sometimes benefit greatly from a sympathetic ear." She smiled faintly. "That's all I'm offering."

Nell let out a quiet sigh of resignation. "I see the news regarding the *Eleanor* is already circulating, then."

"I'm afraid so," said Mei Ling, her expression compassionate. "Word travels swiftly along the waterfront. Is that why you're still here so late?"

Like a wave crashing over her, Nell felt the weight of months of silence and strain. There was something in Mei Ling's gaze, steadfast, discreet, understanding, that made her feel safe enough, in that moment, to speak her truth.

"I'm afraid the business is in trouble," she confessed. "My father had long been battling creditors before he took that commission with the East India Company. He loathed them, but he did it to try and get us back on an even keel."

She paused, then added more quietly, "But now, finding those papers, I can see he's been juggling debts for months... choosing who to pay and who to delay. And the insurance, he was forced to cease the payments. The *Eleanor* wasn't covered when disaster struck. All those poor families..." Her voice faltered momentarily. "I have no idea what I shall say to them when they come seeking what they are rightfully owed."

Mei Ling nodded slowly, her expression thoughtful. Nell could tell she was turning something over in her mind.

"You know," she said at last, "there are other ways to make money when you have ships at your disposal."

Nell's brow creased. "What do you mean?"

"There are certain shipments," Mei Ling said carefully, "that require discretion. Small packages. Highly profitable. Certain conditions must be met, of course, but if the system is meticulously organised. And executed with precision, there is minimal risk to consider."

"I assume what you're suggesting falls outside the bounds of the law," said Nell flatly. "Which means there's always a risk."

"That's true," Mei Ling admitted. "I can't guarantee there won't be any difficulties. But the commodity of which I speak has been transported from China to British shores for many decades. Once it is safely delivered to port, I have a sophisticated distribution network already established. You'd take a cut. Considerable profits that would resolve your immediate financial difficulties. And the names behind the network are... well connected."

"You mean opium," Nell said, her voice barely above a whisper.

Mei Ling gave a small, almost imperceptible nod.

"I couldn't," Nell said firmly. "I'm sorry. More than ever, I understand that sometimes one must profit however one can, but my father is a man of principle. He would be mortified if I were to take the business in that direction. You understand, I hope."

"I do," said Mei Ling. "Please forgive me if I've offended you. I can see you're in a predicament, and I merely wished to offer a potential solution."

"Really, I'm not offended," Nell said with sincerity, reaching across to briefly touch Mei Ling's hand. "I'm grateful for your help, and for your offer, but I just can't do it."

"Of course." Mei Ling rose to leave. "Then allow me to leave you with these herbal treatments. The green packet contains a poultice for your bruising. Apply it warm, twice daily. The red package holds a tea that will ease your pain and help you sleep. And please, do call on me again if you get into any further trouble. Or if you just need someone to listen."

As silently as she had appeared, Mei Ling vanished down the stairs, her footsteps fading into the quiet of the night.

Nell remained seated in the darkness, alone with her thoughts once more. She gathered the documents with trembling hands, returning them to their hiding place. Tomorrow would bring fresh challenges. The grieving families seeking compensation, the creditors circling like vultures, and the threat of that scarred debt collector's return.

But for tonight, she would allow herself the small comfort of Mei Ling's herbal remedies and perhaps a few hours' respite from the crushing burden she now carried.

Gathering her things, Nell locked the office and made her way cautiously down the stairs. She secured the outer office door behind her and stepped out into the fog-thickened London night. The dock was eerily quiet, save for the soft rhythmic lap of the Thames against the moorings and the faint murmur of low voices. Somewhere nearby, a curl of tobacco smoke hung in the air, dockhands loitering among the crates, playing cards and drinking gin, in no apparent hurry to return to their wives.

As she pocketed the office key, Nell glanced toward the warehouse, checking that the workers had remembered to lock up. She saw the padlock fastened securely on the outside of the heavy wooden doors and was about to turn away, satisfied, when something strange made her stop.

She stared more intently at the warehouse door, her brow furrowing.

Something was wrong.

She couldn't place it at first, but then she saw it. A faint orange glow seeping from the crack beneath the door. Frowning, she took a few cautious steps forward. The closer she came, the more she felt it: heat radiating off the wood. The scent of tobacco had vanished, replaced by something sharper, more alarming. Smoke. Not the pleasant aroma of pipes or cigarettes, but the acrid stench of burning wood and merchandise.

Nell hurried forward with mounting trepidation. The door crackled faintly.

She reached for the padlock, but withdrew her hand at once with a sharp cry of pain. It was searing hot to the touch, scorching her fingertips.

Fire.

Her stomach dropped.

"Help! Please, someone, quickly!"

A few dockworkers looked up from their makeshift circle of upturned crates. One of them squinted into the fog.

"Miss Warrington? What are you still doing here? And what's the matter?"

"The warehouse," she called, her voice urgent. "It's on fire!"

Sensing the seriousness in her tone, several of the men abandoned their card game and rushed to her side. One placed a hand on the warehouse door. "You're right, miss. She's burning."

"Stand back, if you please, Miss Warrington," another said with surprising authority, already calling to his companions. "Me and the lads will see to it."

One brawny worker came running with a heavy axe slung over his shoulder, his face grim with determination. With a few powerful, well-aimed swings, he broke the padlock free from its housing, and together they heaved open the massive doors with considerable effort.

A wave of fire surged outwards, belching black smoke and sparks into the sky. Ash and soot swirled through the fog like ink in water.

"Tommy, lad!" one of the older men shouted.

A teenage boy sprang up from behind the crates.

"Run to the station, fetch the fire brigade. Sharpish!"

"Yes, Dad!" the boy called and tore off into the night.

Nell could only stand and watch, heart pounding against her bruised ribs, the heat pressing against her skin as she mentally calculated the contents of the warehouse. Crates of tea, linens, fine porcelain, she could see their charred remains already. *How much will it cost to reimburse the owners? How much more of this can we take?*

The doors hung open wide, and several intrepid workers attempted valiantly to smother the advancing flames with great canvas tarpaulins soaked hastily in water from nearby barrels. As Nell stepped closer, the smoke burning her eyes, something caught her attention. Pinned deliberately to the inside of the warehouse door, just above the flames.

A single playing card.

The jack of spades.

She reached up and plucked it free, slipping it into her coat pocket without thinking. She wasn't sure why, but something told her it was significant.

The minutes dragged into hours as the fire raged on. When the brigade finally arrived, they worked tirelessly to douse the flames. By the early morning, the fire was out, the sky a pale, smoky grey.

Nell stood amidst the smouldering ruins, surveying the blackened, sodden remnants of the once-valuable goods within. Her dress was smeared with soot, her hair had escaped its pins, and exhaustion etched deep lines around her eyes. This latest catastrophe seemed almost deliberately calculated to push the company beyond recovery.

A kindly dockhand, one of the older men who had known her father for many years, approached and placed a gentle hand upon her shoulder.

"Miss... me and the lads'll tidy up what we can. Why don't you go on home and get some proper rest? We'll hold the fort."

She looked up at him, her face streaked with ash and exhaustion.

"Thank you, Mr. Perkins," she said softly, remembering his name from her father's frequent mentions. "That's very kind of you."

"I'll fetch you a carriage, miss."

And for once, Nell was content to be treated like a lady in need of protection in this unforgiving world of men. Her usual fierce independence momentarily surrendered to necessity.

She settled into the seat with a groan of fatigue and let the motion of the carriage carry her away, towards home.

As the cab rattled through the gradually awakening streets of London, she withdrew the playing card from her pocket and examined it in the growing light. The jack of spades, the knave, stared back at her with enigmatic, painted eyes. Someone had deliberately set fire to her warehouse; of that much she was certain. The question that now plagued her was simple: who among her father's enemies had marked the Warrington Shipping Company for destruction?

CHAPTER 3

*H*aving barely slept, Nell was up early and at the docks before most of the hands had arrived. The acrid scent of smoke still lingered in the air as she picked her way through the scorched remains of the small warehouse that had burned in the night.

True to their word, the men had done a thorough job of clearing the worst of it, though the soot-streaked windows and layer of ash upon the floorboards told the full story. She ran her gloved hand along one of the blackened beams, her thoughts drifting back to years before when her father had first expanded the business and added the warehouse to the shipyard.

She had only been a child then, but she remembered the pride in his voice as he walked her through it, giving her a personal tour of what he called "the future of Warrington & Company." He'd even let her help the workmen, staining the beams and painting the gilded sign that once hung proudly over the doors.

"I'm sorry, Papa," she whispered, her breath visible in the cold morning air. "I'll make this right. I promise you."

Her reverie was broken by one of the workers approaching, his tone edged with reluctance.

"If you please, miss, the inspector's here," he said, shifting uncomfortably from one foot to the other.

"The inspector?" she said, surprised.

"Yes, miss. Inspector Hart," he said with a roll of his eyes.

"And he don't miss a thing," added another man from behind. "Known for sniffing out trouble, that one."

Nell sighed, adjusting her clothes. Facing the law was not how she'd hoped to start the day.

"Very well," she said, steeling herself as she moved through the charred remains.

As she emerged from the building, she spotted a

tall, well-dressed man striding toward her with purposeful steps. His sharp eyes darted from side to side, as though cataloguing every detail.

"And you must be Miss Warrington," he said, offering his hand. "Inspector Elijah Hart."

Now that he stood before her, she saw he was more than half a foot taller. Still, she lifted her chin and met his gaze without wavering. Wiping her palm discreetly on her skirts, she took his hand. The touch startled her. It had been months since she'd felt the closeness of another person. Not since embracing her father before he'd left for India.

"I understand you've had some trouble," the inspector said, releasing her hand and extracting a small notebook from his waistcoat pocket.

"Well, I wouldn't quite call it trouble, Inspector," she replied, her voice steadier than she felt. "It seems we've had an unfortunate accident in one of our warehouses."

"An accident, you say?" he echoed, eyes fixed on her face with an intensity that made her wish she'd taken more care with her appearance that morning.

"I believe so, yes," she replied evenly, smoothing back a stray lock of chestnut hair that had escaped her bun.

"Nevertheless, best I have a look at the damaged area.

"Of course. Come this way."

They walked through the warehouse as Hart examined the damage, poking at blackened beams and stirring ash with the toe of his polished boot.

"Your men cleaned up quickly," he observed, one eyebrow arching slightly as he scribbled something in his notebook.

"Yes," Nell replied, uncertain of his tone. "We still have a business to run, Inspector. My father's clients expect their deliveries, fire or no."

"Hmm. I see. And you believe the fire was accidental?"

"I'm afraid I don't know, Inspector," she answered, watching him carefully. "Isn't that your job to determine?"

He gave a tight smile that didn't reach his eyes. "Indeed it is, Miss Warrington. But in my experience, fires like this are rarely random. Someone usually has a reason, or something to gain."

"A very interesting theory," Nell said coolly, though her heart quickened its pace. "Though I can't imagine who would target Warrington & Company."

"You can't?" he asked, his brow rising once again.

That expression was beginning to wear on her nerves. "I understand your father has left the company in... shall we say, precarious circumstances?"

Before she could respond, they rounded a corner near the back of the warehouse just as two dockworkers, unaware of their presence, were mid-argument, their voices echoing against the sooty walls.

"Well, anyone could be careless with the lamps these days," one said hotly, jabbing a finger at his companion's chest. "'Specially with the amount you've been drinking lately."

"Me? Hardly!" the other protested. "I need this place running just as much as you do. I can't afford to miss another week's pay with five mouths to feed at home."

"Some say the miss is in desperate need of the insurance from this," the first man hissed, his voice dropping to a conspiratorial whisper. "What with the bank coming to collect next month."

Nell cleared her throat sharply, her cheeks burning with indignation. The men spun around, faces pale beneath their grime, clearly realising they'd been overheard.

"I think you're needed down at the docks," she

said curtly, her eyes hard. "The Merrimack should be arriving within the hour."

But it was too late. Inspector Hart had heard every word.

He turned to her, his expression unreadable but calculating.

"Might we go to your office, Miss Warrington?" he asked calmly. "Just to conduct a routine check of your paperwork, you understand. Insurance documents, ledgers... that sort of thing."

Nell's heart thudded against her stays. She couldn't refuse. Refusal would only deepen his suspicion. And yet, she knew what he would find in those ledgers. The mounting debts. The loans her father had taken. The desperate measures she'd been considering.

"Of course, Inspector," she said, lifting her chin once more and meeting his gaze with forced composure. "Follow me."

The clack of their footsteps echoed up the wooden stairs as Nell led Inspector Hart into the office. She crossed the room, her tread careful, one hand braced briefly against the desk as she moved behind it.

"Please," she said, gesturing to the chair opposite.

Hart didn't sit. Instead, he wandered the space slowly, taking in the surroundings with a practiced eye. His gaze moved over the worn ledgers, the rows of correspondence, the half-melted candle on the sill.

"I imagine this is your father's office," he said, his voice clipped but not unkind.

"It is," Nell replied. "I've kept it as he left it."

"A strong presence, I imagine."

Nell offered a faint smile. "You could say that."

He stepped toward the window, glancing out across the yard. "I understand he's in India now. Left you to hold the fort."

She bristled at the phrasing. "He didn't *leave* me. He went to pursue an opportunity for the company. I'm simply continuing the work he entrusted me with."

Hart turned, raising an eyebrow. "Indeed. And how have you fared in the meantime?"

"I'm managing."

His gaze lingered on her for a moment longer than necessary. Then, he stepped closer to the desk. "May I see your books? Shipping logs, insurance papers. Routine procedure, of course."

"Of course."

She turned to retrieve them, moving stiffly, with the unmistakable caution of someone nursing pain. When she reached high to grasp a ledger from the top shelf, she faltered, just for a second, and winced, her breath catching.

Hart noticed.

He said nothing at first, watching her with sharpened attention. Then, quietly: "You're hurt."

Nell stilled, her back still to him. "It's nothing."

He waited. "I've seen injuries hidden under fine clothes before. You didn't get that from a falling crate."

Nell turned, face composed but eyes hard. "As I said, Inspector, it's nothing that concerns you."

A silence passed between them. He nodded once, slowly. "Very well."

As she placed the ledgers on the desk, Hart moved closer, flipping open the covers and scanning the contents in silence.

"You've taken on a heavy load, Miss Warrington," he said eventually, running a finger down a column of figures. "Most women would've sold the company and taken a comfortable inheritance."

"I'm not most women," she replied coolly.

"So I see." He glanced at her from under his brow. "You're tougher than you look."

The ticking of the wall clock suddenly seemed louder.

He turned back to the ledger, but not before she saw a flicker of something soften in his expression.

"You've been dealing with creditors," he noted, tapping a page. "Late payments... some quite significant."

"Yes," Nell said simply.

"And yet no active claims filed for the fire."

"We're not currently insured."

"Indeed," Hart said, flipping to the back of the ledger. "Cohen & Cohen withdrew coverage six months ago."

She said nothing, her jaw set.

"You know what the penalty is for submitting a false claim?"

"I haven't submitted anything," she snapped. "And I don't intend to."

"Your loyalty's admirable," he said finally, "but you might find it less lonely if you stopped defending every brick of this place like it was sacred."

"This *place* is all I have," she said quietly. "And until you've built something worth losing, Inspector, don't presume to tell me how to hold it together."

Hart blinked once, almost a flinch, and then

offered a curt nod, a flicker of respect flashing in his gaze.

"I see," he said. "Well. You've been cooperative, Miss Warrington. I appreciate your candour."

She inclined her head slightly.

He stepped back from the desk, brushing a fleck of soot from his cuff. "One final question, Miss Warrington."

"Yes?"

"Have you any enemies?"

She hesitated. "No. Not that I know of."

"Curious, then," Hart said, his voice low. "Fires rarely start without intention. And someone meant to send a message."

She said nothing.

He moved toward the door, then turned back to her one last time. "If someone has... harmed you," he said, his tone softer now, "you should report it."

Nell raised her chin. "Thank you, Inspector. But I can handle myself."

He held her gaze. "I believe you." His lips twitched, just short of a smile. "Good day, Miss Warrington."

And with that, he was gone, leaving her alone in the silence of her office, unsure whether she'd just passed a test, or failed one.

She absentmindedly reached into the pocket of her skirts and drew out the playing card, turning it over between her fingers. Although Inspector Hart had made his suspicions clear, there was something about him, something she couldn't quite name, that made her want to confide in him.

She wondered if she should have told him about the card. Perhaps he'd seen something like it before, something that might shed light on the fire. And yet, to mention it would be to invite further scrutiny onto the blaze, the business, and herself.

But still... the thought of seeing Inspector Hart again was, for some reason, a thrilling one.

Finally, she decided the risk was too great.

She slipped the card into the hidden compartment in the desk, turned the small brass key with a quiet click, and tucked the key back into her pocket.

Rising, she crossed to the window at the far end of the office and looked out across the docks. In the distance, she spotted Hart striding away, his coat catching in the breeze.

Just then, he paused.

He turned.

For the briefest of moments, he looked up directly at her window.

Then he walked on.

Nell stepped back from the glass, unsettled. It seemed she would now have to add the inspector to the ever-growing list of things she needed to worry about.

CHAPTER 4

The morning light was pale over Limehouse, slinking across the cobbles and catching in the puddles left from last night's rain. A grey mist hung over the Thames, obscuring the opposite bank and lending the scene a ghostly quality that matched Nell's mood. She stood by the eastern berth, sleeves rolled, directing the last of the tea crates onto a waiting cart. Her bruises ached in the cold, but she kept her jaw tight and her voice steady. She didn't have the luxury of feeling comfort, not today. Not any day, lately.

"Careful with that!" she barked, as one of the boys swung a crate too hard onto the stack. It wobbled precariously, threatening to send the entire morning's work tumbling down, and then righted itself. The lad flushed and muttered an apology.

She turned away before her face gave her away, tiredness etched in every premature line, the weight of decisions still unmade pressing on her shoulders.

As she looked out over the greyness of the day, a figure caught her eye, conspicuous by the bright peacock blue silk that seemed to brighten the docks as she walked through them. She stood apart from the noise and grit of the dockworkers as if the chaos didn't dare touch her.

"I was just passing," Mei Ling said, as she joined Nell on the dockside.

"Is that so?" said Nell, a small smile on her lips that didn't reach her eyes. "In Limehouse? At seven in the morning?"

"I heard the inspector paid a visit."

"Word travels fast," Nell sighed, pulling her shawl tighter around her shoulders.

"He's clearly suspicious." Mei's eyes flicked to the scorched warehouse wall. "He'll be back. They always come back when they smell fire."

Nell, conscious of the prying eyes and straining ears of the curious dockworkers, some of whom had abandoned all pretence of work to gawp at the elegant Chinese woman, turned towards the office.

"Let's speak inside," she murmured. "I'm sure I can stretch to a cup of tea, though it won't be the quality you're accustomed to."

Upstairs, the women sat on opposite sides of the desk, sipping from the steaming mugs.

"So were you really just passing?" asked Nell, setting down her mug and fixing her visitor with a penetrating stare.

"Well, I just wanted to check that you still had both eyes and all your fingers." she teased, although there was concern in her voice.

"And," she added, meeting Nell's gaze directly, "to say my offer still stands."

Nell stared out at the river. The tide was coming in, slow and thick and brown, the water churning up like the troubles in her head. She sighed heavily.

"I can't," she said, not looking at Mei Ling. "He'll be back soon. My father. And if he ever found out—" Her throat pinched. "He wouldn't understand. He'd think I'd failed him."

"You haven't failed anyone," Mei said quietly. "But you're running out of time to prove it. Your creditors won't wait forever"

"I have to find another way."

Mei inclined her head, the barest nod. She didn't push.

Instead, she said, "You should rest. You look like you've been in a fight with a brick wall."

"I lost," Nell muttered, touching her ribs.

A smile ghosted Mei's lips. "Let me know if you change your mind."

She rose from the desk and left, leaving Nell to her thoughts.

Nell opened the ledger before her, the columns of red ink swimming before her tired eyes as she began to think through the alternative solutions at her disposal, each one more desperate than the last.

Just as Nell was settling down to her ledgers, resigning herself to a day of reviewing and revising figures that refused to balance no matter how she adjusted them, a hesitant knock came at the downstairs door.

Her heart caught in her throat. These days, a visitor to the shipping office rarely brought good news. With a sigh, she set her pen in its holder and rose, smoothing down her skirts.

She picked her way down the stairs and opened the door to find a small woman in threadbare clothing standing on the threshold. An even smaller boy clutched at her faded skirts, half-hidden behind the fabric, his eyes large and wary in his thin face.

"Hello," Nell said gently, noting the darned

elbows of the woman's shawl and the carefully mended tears in her dress. "How can I help you?"

"I'm ever so sorry to disturb you, Miss Warrington," the woman replied, wringing the fabric of her skirt between trembling hands. Her knuckles were red and chapped, bearing the unmistakable marks of laundry work. "My name's Sally Glover. I'm the wife of Bobby Glover—he was a deckhand on the *Eleanor*."

Nell's face tightened as she fought to keep her expression neutral. She nodded and stepped aside, gathering herself.

"Please, come in, Mrs Glover," she said, ushering the woman and child inside. "Won't you come up to my office? Can I offer you some tea? Perhaps the boy would like a biscuit?"

The woman blinked, clearly startled by the politeness.

"No thank you, miss. All the same. I'll be fine," Mrs Glover replied, though the boy's eyes lingered hopefully on the mention of a biscuit.

"Then please, do follow me."

In the office, Nell sat behind her father's desk, while Mrs Glover remained standing, awkward and fidgeting at the threshold.

"Please, Mrs Glover, sit," Nell said gently, indicating

the chair opposite. "And your son as well." She pulled a small footstool from underneath the desk for the child.

"Thank you, miss," the woman replied, lowering herself onto the edge of the chair as if afraid she might soil it. Her posture was stiff, her hands tightly folded in her lap. The boy perched on the stool, his feet swinging nervously above the floor.

"Firstly, I want to say how deeply sorry I am for your loss," Nell said. "I'm incredibly grateful for your husband's service. I can only imagine how you're feeling."

"Thank you, miss," Mrs Glover murmured, her eyes fixed on the floor. "That's kind of you to say. My Bobby always said what a fine man your father is, and how much he respected him. Said Mr Warrington treated his men fair, not like some of the other captains down at the docks."

Nell inclined her head, not trusting her voice. Her father was many things, some admirable, others less so, but he did indeed care for his crew.

The woman fell silent again, clearly struggling to broach the reason for her visit.

"How can I help you today, Mrs Glover?" Nell asked gently.

"Well, miss..." the woman began, twisting the

worn gold band on her finger. "It's just... we've not yet received the compensation that was promised after the Eleanor went down, and I wondered when it might come." Her voice grew smaller with each word. "The parish relief isn't enough, you see."

Nell's heart sank. She had known, of course, that this was likely why the woman had come, but part of her had hoped otherwise. Her father's desperate attempts to keep the business afloat had left him cutting corners, and the consequences were now sitting before her with hungry eyes.

"I'm sorry to ask, miss," the woman continued, glancing down at the boy beside her. "It's just—I've three more at home, and they're all hungry. Young Thomas here is the oldest, just turned eight." The boy straightened slightly at the mention of his age, a flash of pride crossing his pinched features."

"Of course," Nell said quickly, working to keep her voice steady. "I completely understand. I'm afraid the paperwork is being... delayed at the insurance office. They tend to double and triple check everything before releasing funds, you see."

Mrs Glover's shoulders drooped, the brief hope in her eyes extinguished.

"Yes, miss," she said faintly.

She half-rose, clearly intending to leave, but paused, gathering courage.

"I'm sorry, Miss Warrington. Ever so sorry to bring this to your door. We're not beggars. Bobby would turn in his watery grave if he heard me asking for charity. But we are hungry. And when my children are crying in the night for want of food, I'm afraid I'm not too proud to beg."

Nell's throat tightened painfully as she watched the woman's dignity war with her desperation.

"Please don't apologise, Mrs Glover," she said softly. "There's no shame in caring for your children."

Guilt curdled in her stomach. How many families had been left in this position because of her father's financial choices? How many knocks at the door would she have to answer before this was over?

Her hands trembled slightly as she opened the drawer of the desk and drew out the cash box. She counted out what little was inside. Notes and coins, meagre but something, and placed them into an envelope.

"Please accept this for now," Nell said, standing and offering it. "It's all I have here at the office—I'll need to visit the bank for more. But I hope it will be enough to feed your family until the paperwork is completed."

Mrs Glover accepted the envelope and stood, her voice thick. "Thank you, miss. We're ever so grateful. I didn't expect... that is, I hoped..."

She glanced down at the small boy beside her, whose wide eyes were ringed with the unmistakable shadows of hunger and sleepless nights.

"Papa said you were a lady," the boy said suddenly, his voice small but clear. "Said you came to the docks sometimes and always knew the sailors' names."

Nell felt tears prick behind her eyes and blinked them back hastily.

"Your papa was a good man, Thomas," she replied, reaching into the tin on her desk and extracting a barley sugar, which she offered to him. "And very brave."

The boy accepted the sweet as if he'd been given something precious beyond imagining.

"It's quite all right," Nell said to Mrs Glover, who was stammering further thanks. "And please, if you need anything else before the insurance comes through, don't hesitate to return."

"Thank you, Miss Warrington," the woman said

again, clutching the envelope to her chest as if afraid it might vanish. "God bless you."

When the door closed behind them, Nell sank heavily into her chair, fighting back the wave of despair that threatened to engulf her.

How many more families? How many more knocks on the door?

Panic stirred in her chest, creeping in like a rising tide. She stood abruptly and reached for her coat from the hook.

I have to do something.

She caught sight of her reflection in the small looking-glass above the hearth. Taking a steadying breath, she smoothed her hair, replaced the pearl hairpins, and fastened the buttons of her coat.

A visit to the bank requires one to look respectable, she thought grimly, as she stepped outside to hail a carriage.

The banking hall on Lime Street always smelled of wax and self-importance. The marble floors gleamed beneath the gaslight, reflecting the severe faces of men who measured human worth in columns and figures. Nell stood at the counter, spine straight, hands folded so tightly her fingernails had carved half-moons into her palms.

Mr. Hadley took his time. He never rushed, especially not for her. His ink-stained fingers flicked slowly through her father's accounts, mouth pursed as if the ledgers offended him personally. Each turn of a page was deliberate, measured, a small reminder of who held power in this exchange.

"It's irregular," he said at last, not looking up.

Nell fought the urge to lean forward and slap the book shut.

"You've dealt with my father for nearly twenty years," she said instead, keeping her voice controlled.

"Indeed. Mr. Warrington was until fairly recently always prompt and thorough in his business affairs. But as I'm sure you're aware, circumstances have...changed."

Nell swallowed. "I'm asking for an extension on the line of credit. Just six weeks. We've had... a setback."

He clicked his tongue, finally meeting her eyes. "The Eleanor."

"Yes."

"A tragedy, certainly. Twenty-six souls lost, if the reports are accurate. But unfortunate events don't change policy. The bank cannot extend further credit without sufficient collateral."

Nell's jaw tightened. "I have incoming shipments due from Calcutta and Singapore. I can repay—"

"You can promise," Hadley interrupted. "You've already borrowed against your warehouse, and the insurance for that won't cover the loss in full, assuming it pays out at all. There's very little left to secure against."

Nell felt heat creep up her neck. "The crew that died, there are families who've lost everything. I gave them what I could from my own pocket. If you'd just extend—"

Hadley's face turned faintly sympathetic. The way one might look at a wounded dog before putting it down.

"You're admirable, Miss Warrington. Truly. But emotion doesn't balance books. Perhaps it's time to consider letting the business go. Selling off what remains while there's still value to be had. A woman like yourself... I'm sure you'd find some charitable enterprise better suited to your strengths. Teaching, perhaps. Or companion work."

The words landed like slaps. Her throat burned. She forced herself to nod once, as if he'd merely given her the weather forecast.

"I see."

"I can recommend a solicitor who deals with estates in transition," he offered, too brightly. "Mr. Finch on Threadneedle Street is most efficient at these matters. He could have everything settled within a fortnight."

A fortnight. Two weeks to dismantle generations of Warrington pride and ambition. Two weeks to surrender.

She turned and left without another word.

Outside, the sky had opened up, soaking the streets with a steady, cold rain. She pulled her shawl tighter and strode blindly forward, boots slapping through puddles.

The humiliation burned, but beneath it was something worse. A kind of stunned disbelief. *Let it go.* Just like that. Sell everything her father had built, everything she had bled to keep afloat, for what? A pat on the head? A placement in some parish registry to hand out blankets?

She passed the shops and people going about their business as though the world wasn't about to end. A governess shepherding two small children through the downpour. A flower seller hunched miserably beneath an awning, her blooms drooping in the damp. All of them with purposes, with places to be. None of them carrying the weight of twenty-six dead sailors and their hungry children.

Her cheeks were wet, not just from the rain, as she wiped at them with the back of her gloved hand.

By the time she stopped walking, she was halfway through Whitechapel and her skirts were soaked to the knees.

Think, she told herself. *Find another option.*

But the bank had refused her. The insurance company had refused her. The sailors' families would be back soon, asking, hoping, pleading. She had nothing to give them. Nothing left to pawn or promise.

The Eleanor was gone. Her father was half a world away. And she was alone.

She stood beneath the overhang of a shuttered seamstress' shop, fists clenched in the folds of her shawl. The only light nearby flickered behind the frosted window of the apothecary on the corner. Mei Ling's apothecary. How had she found herself here?

For a long time, she stared at it.

Then she moved, her decision made somewhere beyond conscious thought.

Her hand trembled as she reached for the handle. The door creaked open. Warmth spilled out. Lamplight and the comforting smell of herbs, ginger, and exotic spices she couldn't name.

Mei looked up from the counter. She was bottling tinctures, calm and steady. She was dressed more simply than she had been that morning, the peacock blue replaced by a practical black silk embroidered with subtle silver threads. Her gaze met Nell's without surprise, as if she'd been expecting her.

Nell stepped inside, closed the door behind her, and said softly, flatly:

"One shipment. That's all."

Mei set down her dropper, wiped her hands on a cloth, and studied Nell's face, taking in the rain-soaked appearance, the rigid posture, the desperation she couldn't quite conceal.

"Then let's begin."

CHAPTER 5

It was an eerily silent morning as Nell hurried through the streets towards the apothecary. The usual clamour of London, hawkers' cries, carriage wheels on cobblestones, the constant hum of commerce, seemed muffled, as if the city itself were holding its breath. She'd decided against using a carriage to ensure the utmost discretion, a decision she was now regretting as her feet ached in her boots.

Once she arrived at the narrow building wedged between a tobacconist and a pawnbroker, she slipped down the side alley and tapped lightly on the wooden gate three times, as Mei Ling had instructed.

Rain ran in rivulets down the gutters, making the

city seem blurred around the edges somehow. Nell pulled her hood closer around her face, conscious that even at this early hour, eyes might be watching from curtained windows.

After a moment, the gate creaked open and Mei Ling appeared and motioned for her to follow, wordless, through the small courtyard garden where medicinal herbs grew in neat rows, and into the back room of the apothecary.

Inside, the air was warm with the scent of ginger root and something darker—something chemical, metallic.

The shelves were lined with jars. Powdered rhubarb, camphor, valerian, and at the far end, a box sat on the counter. Small. Sealed. Unremarkable, yet somehow the focus of the entire room.

Mei studied her closely as she stood, her shawl dripping from the early morning rain, creating a small puddle on the polished wooden floor.

"You walked?" she questioned, a hint of surprise in her voice.

Nell nodded, removing her sodden gloves. "I thought it best. Cab drivers remember faces, especially at unusual hours."

"You're learning," said Mei Ling, an eyebrow raised in approval. She moved to a small brass jug and poured steaming tea into two delicate cups without handles. "Drink this. You're shivering."

Nell accepted the cup gratefully, the heat seeping into her numb fingers. The tea was bitter but warming, nothing like the sweetened brew served in English parlours.

"Let's get down to business. You'll receive four crates," she said, her voice even. "They're already aboard the *Changzhi*. It left Amoy twelve days ago. Should reach Limehouse in the next day or two, barring delays."

Nell stepped closer to the counter, her heartbeat thudding harder with each step. "What's in them?"

"Tea. Silk. Medicine." Mei lifted the lid of the small box. Inside, neatly packed in straw, was a single wrapped parcel. Small, square, the colour of unpolished amber. "And this."

Nell stared. It looked like nothing. A bundle of pressed wax and linen. It could've been incense. Or herbs. Or poison.

Mei slid it toward her. "We ship it from Fujian in small quantities. Concealed in false-bottom crates. Your job is to receive it quietly, route it to the correct dock, and ensure no one else lays eyes on it. That's all."

Nell blinked, her head still trying to make sense

of how things had got to this point. A month ago, she had been a respectable shipping merchant's daughter. Now she stood in a Chinese apothecary before dawn, agreeing to smuggle opium.

"It'll arrive as part of your father's usual cargo," Mei continued. "Marked with your house seal. Same paper. Same rope. Everything above suspicion."

Nell reached out and picked up the parcel. It was heavier than it looked.

She turned it in her hands, thumb brushing over the seam. "And if someone checks?"

"They won't." Mei's expression didn't shift. "But if they do"—Mei's hand moved to a small drawer under the counter. She pulled it open and took out a thin slip of ivory-coloured paper. Folded inside was a wax seal, stamped with a red handprint.

"If it comes to that," Mei said, placing it gently in Nell's palm, "show them this. Don't explain. Just let them see it."

Nell frowned. "What does it mean?"

"That you're under protection. That this is Jade Hand business." She looked Nell square in the eye. "And that anyone interfering would be... unwise."

Nell swallowed. She folded the paper back up and tucked it into the inner pocket of her coat.

"And after it arrives?"

"A man will collect it within twenty-four hours. You don't need to know his name. Just that he's punctual, and quiet."

Nell let out a breath, stepped back from the counter. "So I'm just a stop on the road."

Mei didn't smile, but her eyes flicked over Nell, seemingly assessing if she was up to the job. "You're a necessary port. And you've already agreed."

Nell nodded once. Her coat still dripped onto the floor, the quiet patter of water on wood the only sound in the room.

"You'll be paid once the shipment clears Limehouse," Mei added. "No delays. No fuss. Enough to cover the compensation for your sailors' families, with some left over to keep the business afloat a while longer."

Outside, the wind had picked up, rattling the glass. Nell imagined the *Changzhi*, cutting through grey waters like a ghost ship, its cargo slumbering in the hold.

"If you're caught," Mei said, her voice suddenly gentler, "deny everything. Say you knew nothing of what was hidden. I'll ensure there's no evidence to link you to us."

Nell looked up sharply. "Is that meant to comfort me?"

Mei's lips curved in the barest suggestion of a smile. "It's meant to be practical. Like you, Miss Warrington."

Two days later, Nell stood shivering on the eastern dock as the *Chang Zai* slipped into port beneath a slate-grey sky. A bitter wind blew off the Thames, stinging her cheeks and numbing her fingers even through her gloves. She had forgone breakfast, her stomach too knotted with anxiety to manage even tea and toast.

She had requested all hands be present for the unloading. Every crate was to be off the ship and into the warehouse as efficiently and quietly as possible. No mistakes. No attention. The men had seemed surprised by her insistence but complied readily enough when she mentioned a bonus for quick work.

Standing at the base of the gangplank, she clutched the manifest and checked each crate with meticulous care, ticking them off one by one. Her eyes scanned constantly for the four particular crates that would be marked with a small, almost invisible red dot at the corner of the shipping label. So far, nothing.

A dockhand strolled over, whistling loudly to himself, the bright noise jangling against her already frayed nerves. He was young, perhaps eighteen, with a shock of ginger hair visible beneath his cap.

"Miss Warrington," he called, squinting up at the ship. "This old girl one of ours, then? Don't recall seeing her before."

"No, Alfie," she replied sharply, without looking up. "It's not a Warrington vessel. I'm doing a favour for a friend. Their ship was diverted from Southampton, so I've arranged for the cargo to come through us instead."

"Sounds interesting," Alfie chirped, rocking back on his heels. "Foreign ship, ain't she? Chinese by the look. Don't see many of those in Limehouse proper."

"It really isn't," Nell snapped, the cold and her fraying patience tipping her tone into something harsher than intended. "Now, kindly get on with your work. I'd like this done before we all freeze to death."

Alfie muttered an apology, pulled his cap down over his ears, and shuffled away, stung by her uncharacteristic brusqueness.

Relieved, Nell returned to her checking, until that infernal whistling started up again, this time from a different direction.

Her head snapped up. "Alfie!"

But he was nowhere in sight.

Across the way, leaning casually against a lamp-post, was a tall, swarthy-looking man. He was the source of the whistling now, and as she caught his eye, he doffed his cap and winked, revealing a shock of dark unruly curls.

How rude, she thought, assuming him to be one of the dockhands shirking his duties.

She gave him a sharp, disapproving look, expecting it would be enough to send him back to work. But instead, he merely smiled wider, thrust his hands deeper into his coat pockets, and lit a cigarette.

Irritated by his impertinence and growing increasingly cold and anxious as more crates appeared from the Changzhi's hold, Nell strode towards him, her boots clicking on the damp stones.

"I'm sorry, I don't recognise you. Are you new here?" she asked, crisp and clipped, drawing herself up to her full height, which still left her looking up at him.

"Me?" the man grinned, revealing teeth that were surprisingly white and even. His eyes, she noticed now, were a startling shade of green against his darker complexion. "I've been around for years, love."

She stiffened at the familiarity, yet found herself

unable to look away from his face. There was something both dangerous and compelling about him, like looking over the edge of a high cliff.

"If you've worked here for some time, then surely you're aware that I don't tolerate cigarette breaks during unloading."

He gave a hearty chuckle, the sound echoing off the brick and water. The cigarette dangled from his lips as he spoke, his accent a curious blend of East End roughness with occasional flashes of something more refined.

"Oh, I don't work for you, miss," he said, removing the cigarette and exhaling a cloud of smoke that drifted between them. "I don't work for anyone."

Nell blinked, taken aback by his boldness. Her gaze flickered involuntarily to his hands. Strong, capable, with a thin white scar running across the knuckles of his right hand. Not the hands of a gentleman, despite the coat.

"Then what are you doing here?" she demanded, suddenly aware of how alone they were at this end of the dock.

"Just observing," he said with a casual shrug. His eyes, those unsettling green eyes, moved from her face down to the manifest she clutched, then back up again, assessing. "Part of my job, being aware when new ventures are afoot, if you get my meaning."

She fought to keep the colour from rising further in her cheeks, aware that he was watching her reaction closely. Her heart hammered uncomfortably against her ribs. "I'm sure I don't."

Another laugh, deeper this time, as if he found her genuinely amusing. "I'm sure you don't, miss."

He stepped away from the lamppost, his eyes lingering on her just a fraction too long. "All I'll say is, be careful with new ventures. Not everyone's as helpful as they seem."

And with that, he turned and strolled off, whistling again as if he hadn't a care in the world, though she noticed his gaze sweeping the dock with careful attention. Not careless at all, then. Simply wanting to appear so.

Nell stood frozen, watching his retreating back, her mind racing. Who was he? What did he know?

She forced herself to turn away, annoyed at her own reaction. She had more important matters at hand than mysterious men with impertinent smiles and eyes that seemed to see too much. The four crates still hadn't appeared, and time was slipping away.

Already rattled, Nell's stomach dropped further

as she spotted Inspector Elijah Hart coming around the corner of the warehouse, heading directly towards her. His tall figure was unmistakable even at a distance.

The panic she'd just fought back surged again, clawing at her throat. She glanced over her shoulder. Several crates still sat exposed on the dock, not yet moved to the warehouse. Only the last few were coming off the Changzhi now, and they were still far from being secured.

And amongst them, she was certain, were the four that could destroy everything.

"Inspector Hart," Nell said, striving to keep her voice calm. "Back so soon?"

"Miss Warrington," he replied, inclining his head with a polite nod. "How are you?"

She met his gaze. His eyes were as alert as ever, yet something in them had changed, less guarded, less steely. There was a softness there today that caught her off guard.

"I'm well," she said cautiously, her tone carefully measured.

He removed his hat and held it in his hands, fingers lightly worrying the brim. "I was in the area," he began, glancing down at the toes of his perfectly polished boots. "I just… wanted to check in. After last time."

He cleared his throat and added, almost reluctantly, "I think perhaps I was harder on you than I needed to be."

Nell blinked, surprised. The warmth of his concern unsettled her more than his sharp questioning ever had.

Of all people, it was the inspector who had returned with an apology when it was she who now had something to hide.

Determined to keep the conversation brief, she offered a polite, deflecting smile. "It's of no consequence, Inspector Hart. You were doing your duty. And, as you can imagine," she added with a flicker of dry humour, "I'm quite accustomed to harsher treatment."

He looked at her intently, his brow furrowing as if he could see the truth beneath her composed surface.

"I don't doubt it," he said quietly. "And you cope with it… admirably, Miss Warrington."

She inclined her head slightly, unsure how to respond. She felt suddenly too aware of the cold, of the wind brushing against her cheeks, of his eyes still resting on her.

"Thank you," she said at last, her voice softer than she intended.

They both turned instinctively to watch the final crates being unloaded from the *Chang Zai*. As she monitored the movement, Nell caught his gaze still lingering on her. Not as a policeman scrutinising a suspect, but as a man studying something he hadn't expected to care about.

"You seem tired," he said after a moment. "I hope the fire and… the rest hasn't left you with more than bruises."

She paused, her breath catching slightly.

"Really, Inspector," she said, summoning a smile. "I'm quite fine. But thank you for your concern. As you can see, I'm rather busy."

There was a note of dismissal in her voice, and he seemed to catch it. He returned his hat to his head and turned to leave, pausing after only a few steps.

When he turned back to her, something in his expression had softened even further. Less duty, more something else.

"I meant what I said, Miss Warrington. I'm here to help. If anything happens… you can come to me."

Nell's jaw tightened, the guilt rising in her throat like bile. She hadn't told him about the smuggled cargo. About the playing card. About the man by the lamppost.

But her face remained composed, unreadable. She gave a small nod.

"Thank you, Inspector."

Then she turned on her heel and walked briskly toward the crates, leaving him standing there, watching her go.

CHAPTER 6

The morning fog rolled in thick over Limehouse, swallowing the rooftops and providing a welcome blanket of obscurity. Nell stood beside the cart, one gloved hand resting on the edge of the nearest crate. Four in total, each marked in her father's neat stamp: *Warrington Shipping Co.*—a lie in wood and ink.

The driver, a squat man with shoulders like barrels, tightened the reins with a grunt. He hadn't spoken a word since arriving at half-past four, and Nell didn't ask his name. Mei had said he was loyal, and in this world, that meant more than charming.

She pulled her cloak tighter around her shoulders and gave a sharp nod.

"Go."

The cart creaked to life, wheels bumping over the uneven cobbles. The mist made everything feel quieter than it should've been, like the city had taken a breath and forgotten to exhale.

They turned down a narrow lane past the butcher's, cut through alleys that stank of wet coal and rotting potatoes, and finally emerged onto a broader road running alongside the Regent's Canal. A cold wind whipped up off the water. The driver halted with a low whistle between his teeth.

The wharf was nearly deserted, save for two men waiting by a barge moored to the stone steps. Faces obscured beneath caps and scarves wound high against the morning chill, they moved with the kind of purpose that required no conversation. The taller one's eyes flicked briefly toward Nell before dismissing her as irrelevant.

She should have been offended. Instead, relief washed through her.

Nell watched as the driver unloaded each crate, sliding them into the open hull with practised ease. No one spoke. No one looked at her. When the last crate disappeared into the barge's hold, one of the men offered a single nod before stepping back into shadow.

It was over in minutes. Too fast. Too smooth. Like a performance rehearsed a hundred times.

As the boat pushed off, cutting a slow ripple across the still canal, Nell's breath caught.

This is real now. You're part of it.

She waited until the barge was nearly gone before turning back toward the alley. The driver had already disappeared, cart and all, leaving no trace of their transaction. The street behind her lay empty, windows still shuttered against the dawn.

Just as well. She didn't want witnesses.

She walked the whole way back to the warehouse alone. A constable passed her near the grocer's, tipping his hat in that automatic way they always did to respectable ladies, although Nell wasn't sure if that's what she was anymore. Not after this morning's business.

She nodded, kept walking, eyes forward as though she belonged exactly where she was.

But her stomach churned.

Not because he'd looked at her.

Because for a moment, she'd been afraid he wouldn't.

She rounded the corner onto the docks, and picked her way through stacked crates towards her office. Once inside, she shut it behind her with a soft thud, turning the brass key in the lock with trembling fingers. The river was quiet now, the mist still hanging thick along the windows.

The office was dim, the oil lamp guttering low on her father's desk. As she moved to sit down, something pale caught her eye just under the doorframe.

An envelope.

No name. No seal. Just plain paper, folded precisely.

She stared at it for a moment before picking it up. It was heavier than it looked.

She opened the envelope to see crisp notes. Clean. Counted. She ran her thumb over the edges. The stack was tight, the paper cool and stiff. More money than she'd seen in one place since her father's departure.

She sat down heavily in the chair, the one he used to sit in when tallying up shipments and counting barrels of rum with a pencil between his teeth. She placed the envelope on the desk, directly beside the open ledger. The entries from yesterday still lay bare. Her spidery handwriting next to his careful, looping script.

Her throat tightened. This wasn't how he did business.

This wasn't how *she* did business.

She pushed back from the desk abruptly and stood, pacing the office. She looked out the window. Nothing but fog and the vague yellow glow of the distant gas lamps near the quay. The world felt further away than ever, as though London itself had abandoned her to this half-life of compromise and quiet desperation.

You did it for the right reasons.

She turned back to the desk. The envelope sat there like an accusation, intensifying her regret.

This keeps the doors open. You can make sure he still has a business to return to.

She sat again and pressed her fingertips to her temple, where a headache was beginning to form.

It was just one shipment.

The words rang in her head like a lie whispered too many times.

She reached across the desk and pulled open the drawer. Inside lay the red paper Mei had given her. The sigil of protection, stamped with the mark of the Jade Hand. It lay nestled against her father's pocket watch and an old brass compass that no longer worked.

She picked up the symbol and tried to imagine what he would say if he saw it.

Would he understand? Or would his face twist

with disappointment? Would he recognise the same determination that had built his business from nothing, or would he see only the sharp edges of her compromise?

A sharp knock at the downstairs door shattered the stillness.

She jumped, nearly knocking over the ink pot. Stared at the envelope. Then at the drawer with its damning contents.

She closed it with shaking fingers, pushed the money beneath the ledger, and hurried down the stairs.

Nell opened the office door to find a young woman, around her own age, standing in the doorway, soaked through by the clinging morning fog. Beside her was a little girl, no older than five, her teeth chattering as the cold mist swirled around her. The woman's worn cloak hung heavy with moisture, water dripping steadily onto the threshold.

She looked up apologetically, brushing droplets of water from her lashes.

"I'm ever so sorry, Miss Warrington, for disturbing you at this hour," she said, her voice trembling.

Grateful for a distraction from her troubled thoughts, Nell stepped aside and welcomed them in.

"Please don't apologise. Come in, it's bitter out there," she said gently, ushering them inside and shutting the door behind them.

"How can I help you?"

"Well, miss... my Charlie—he was a deckhand on the *Eleanor*, you understand."

Nell's expression shifted with quiet sympathy. "I see. I'm terribly sorry for your loss. How have you been managing?"

The woman hesitated, wringing her hands. "That's just it, miss. We ain't been, not really. I'm Lydia Harris, and this is my Molly." She gave the child a small, affectionate glance. "Charlie was the eldest, my only child of working age. There's just me and my husband now, and he's too sick to work. The consumption, miss. We're... well, miss, we're at a loss."

Nell nodded solemnly, her heart twisting. The crates she'd sent down the canal that morning suddenly seemed very far away, a different life, a different kind of desperation. "Let me put the kettle on," she said, "You both look half-frozen."

She disappeared briefly into the back room where a small stove burned low. She stoked it higher, added coal from the dwindling supply, and set the kettle to boil. While she waited, she found clean mugs and added a generous spoonful of sugar to each, a luxury she normally wouldn't afford, but which seemed essential now. She returned with two steaming mugs of tea, fragrant with the last of her Ceylon leaves.

"Let's go upstairs to the office," she said. "It's warmer up there."

They climbed the stairs together, and Nell led them into the office, placing the mugs gently in front of Lydia and her daughter.

"Please, drink," she said. "It's hot."

Lydia stared at the tea as though she'd never expected such kindness.

"Here," Nell said, turning to the little girl. "I've put a bit of extra sugar in yours. That should perk you up."

Molly glanced at her mother, who gave a small nod. The girl took the mug with both hands, cradling it gratefully as the warmth spread through her tiny fingers.

"As I said, Miss Warrington, I'm sorry to trouble you. Sally Glover said you were helping some of the families. I just wondered..." Lydia trailed off, clearly uncomfortable. "I just wondered if there was any word—any help. We'd be ever so grateful for something to buy food... and coal."

Nell thought of the envelope, delivered just an hour ago. Payment for services rendered.

"Of course," Nell said brightly, her voice warmer than she felt. "I've just made some progress on that. Bear with me."

She opened the drawer and took out the envelope that had become both a burden and a lifeline. But in this moment, looking at Molly's wan face and Lydia's desperate hope, it looked like a blessing. She drew out several notes, counted them with steady fingers, and held them out to Lydia.

The woman's eyes widened in disbelief. Then her shoulders crumpled, and she burst into tears. Great, heaving sobs of relief that shook her frame.

"Oh, Miss Warrington, you've no idea what this means to us," she said, pressing the notes to her chest as though afraid they might vanish. "Molly, look! Look what Miss Warrington's gave us! It's more money than we've ever seen. What shall we have for supper, eh? Perhaps a bit of mutton? And coal enough to warm the whole house!"

The little girl's eyes lit up at the question, her thin face beaming with sudden joy.

Eager to leave and fill their bellies, Lydia rose from her seat, and Nell did the same, stepping forward to gently clasp the woman's hand.

"It's quite alright," Nell said. "Truly. It's the least I can do under the circumstances."

Having drained the last of her tea, the little girl ran forward and flung her arms around Nell's legs in a fierce hug, her small face pressed against the fabric of Nell's skirt.

"Molly!" her mother scolded, though her tone was light. "Don't go bothering Miss Warrington—"

Nell laughed, for the first time in what felt like months.

"It's quite alright," she said softly, resting her hand on the child's head. "I'm just happy I could help. In some small way."

As the Harris family left the office, Nell gently closed the door behind them.

She returned to the desk, where the drawer still lay open, the paper with the Jade Hand's mark catching the dim light. She picked it up again, running her thumb over the raised symbol.

And for a brief, fragile moment, the compromises she had made felt worth it.

She closed the drawer with quiet resolution. Perhaps this was how her father had begun—small compromises for greater goods. Perhaps there was a way through this labyrinth that didn't end in ruin.

Later that day, she was halfway through checking

the bolts on the warehouse doors when she felt it, that subtle shift in the air, like a current turning. A prickle ran up the back of her neck.

"You always this thorough, or just playing hard to get?"

Nell turned, slowly.

Jonny Collins stood a few paces behind her, one boot perched on a low crate, arms folded, wearing the same grin he had no doubt been born with. Lazy, lopsided, and far too self-satisfied for her liking. His dark hair curled rebelliously over his forehead, and those green eyes glittered with amusement.

"I didn't hear you," she said coolly.

"That's sort of the point." He stepped down and sauntered closer, hands in his coat pockets. "You looked busy. Didn't want to startle you."

"You never could," she said with an air of assurance she didn't feel.

His grin widened. "You wound me, Nell."

"If only," she retorted, rolling her eyes.

He looked around the dock as if appraising it. "Quiet today. Fog's got everything wrapped up like a secret. Seems fitting."

She turned back to the lock, deliberately slow. "If you came here to talk weather, I'm busy."

"Oh, come on. Don't be like that." He leaned

against the wall beside her. "Can't a man pay a compliment?" he asked, taking a step closer. "Your little operation yesterday? Beautiful. Smooth. Clockwork. It's like you've been running quiet trades your whole life."

Her spine stiffened, a dread settling in her stomach. "I don't know what you think you saw—"

"I didn't say I saw anything. You did." He shot her a sideways glance, lips twitching. "You're not very good at lying, by the way. Not yet."

Nell clenched her jaw. "Why are you really here?"

"To offer you something." He pushed off the wall and faced her fully. "Protection. Advice. Company, if you're the brooding type."

"I'm the 'leave me alone' type." She glared at him, but he only chuckled. The sound was maddening.

She raised an eyebrow, deciding to play his game. "So you're offering protection?"

"A watchful eye," he said, tilting his head. "A few quiet words in the right places. You wouldn't believe how quickly a misplaced crate can grow legs. Or how many men are just dying to find out what you're moving through those tea shipments of yours."

She said nothing, unwilling to confirm his suspicions.

He stepped closer. "You've got talent, Nell. Brains. Guts. But you're walking into a world where good intentions get chewed up and spat out faster than you can say 'ledger.' I'm offering to keep the wolves off your door, for a small piece of the pie."

She looked up at him then, properly. There was mischief in his smile, yes, but something else too. He wasn't merely an opportunist; he was dangerous. And worst of all, he knew it.

"There's people watching, Nell. Not just me. Not just the nice ones. You're in deeper than you think, and this city doesn't take kindly to independents getting clever."

"I'm not clever," she said, hating how defensive she sounded. "Just desperate."

His expression flickered, something almost like admiration. "Desperate's dangerous. That's when people get bold. And bold people either get rich… or get disappeared."

She narrowed her eyes, refusing to be intimidated. "Is that supposed to scare me?"

"Would it work if it was?"

They stood in silence for a beat, the distance between them charged. Then his gaze dropped briefly to her mouth, just for a second, before snapping back to her eyes. He smiled again, slower this time.

"I could help you, you know. Make things… easier."

"I've survived just fine on my own."

"You've scraped by. There's a difference." He stepped forward, close now, too close. "And it's okay to want more."

"I don't want anything you have to offer."

His smile didn't falter. "I didn't say you did. But you might. Eventually." There was certainty in his voice that both irritated and intrigued her.

Her cheeks flushed, infuriatingly so. She turned back to the crate.

He moved to leave, pausing at the edge of the mist.

"Think about it," he said, voice lighter now. "You might not trust me but at least you know where I stand. Can't say the same for everyone else on this dock."

She didn't answer.

"Oh," he added, glancing back at her with a wink that was entirely too familiar, "don't look so serious. You're doing fine. One hell of a debut."

And then he was gone, swallowed by the fog as completely as if he'd never been there at all.

Nell stood motionless for a long time, heart still beating too fast.

She wasn't sure what scared her more. That he knew too much. Or that she wanted to see more of him.

CHAPTER 7

The Islington house was quiet in the early hours, the kind of quiet that made Nell's footsteps echo too loudly down the hallway. She hadn't been home in three nights. Too much to do at the warehouse. Too much to avoid here, in these rooms that still breathed with her father's absence.

The drawing room hadn't changed. The brass clock ticked steadily on the mantel. A thin layer of dust lined the windowsill where the maid, now only coming twice weekly, another economy, hadn't reached. Her father's favourite chair sat by the grate, still bearing the faint indent of his last sitting, though that had been nearly a year ago now.

With a weary sigh, she dropped the small bundle of post on the writing desk, collected from the hall table where it had accumulated in her absence. Most of it was useless, bills with red stamps declaring urgency, a crumpled leaflet for a political meeting at the Mechanics' Institute, something in her father's name from the bank with its imposing crest. She didn't want to open that one. Not yet. Perhaps not ever

The last envelope made her pause.

Thin, worn. From India. The stamps exotic and colourful against the creamy paper, the postmark smudged from its long journey.

Her chest tightened.

She broke the seal with careful fingers, unfolding the letter slowly like it might tear. The handwriting made her throat ache. Looping and neat, a little heavier now with age but unmistakably his. Seeing it was like hearing his voice after all these months.

"Dearest Nell,

I hope this finds you safe and well. Every time your last letter arrives, I begin counting the days until the next. You sound tired, sweetheart. Don't wear yourself to the bone in my absence. Remember what I always told you— the ships will sail whether we fret or not. The sea keeps her own counsel."

She stopped, fingers trembling slightly. Her

father's little sayings. How she'd missed them. Her breath caught in her throat as she continued

"The heat here is relentless. Even the insects seem to move more slowly, as if swimming through treacle. But the opportunity is worth the discomfort. The owners are eager for new shipping contracts, and mention of the Warrington name still carries weight, thank God.

You're doing something remarkable. Keeping the business afloat, managing those unruly boys on the docks. I don't know how you've done it. But I'm proud. Do you hear me, Nell? Proud. Of every decision you've made.

When I return, it will be with a new contract and the money to put everything right. But you've done more than I ever expected. More than I ever could.

Be kind to yourself. Rest when you can. You're stronger than you think.

All my love, Father."

She read it twice.

Then again.

The final lines blurred as her eyes stung.

She folded the paper neatly and laid it beside the envelope from Mei, still thick with the cash she couldn't bear to spend, even after helping the Harris widow. It sat there like it had grown heavier in her absence, a physical manifestation of her compromise.

The fire crackled in the grate half-heartedly. She thought about throwing Mei's envelope in. Just tossing it on the flames, letting it curl and blacken and vanish. One movement and she could pretend none of it had happened.

But her hand didn't move.

He's proud of you.

The words made her feel sick. Her father, halfway around the world, thinking she'd upheld his honour and preserved his name through honest industry and clever management. Meanwhile, she was slipping crates of poison through Limehouse like some low-level dockland broker. Being watched by men like Jonny Collins, whose interest felt both threatening and thrilling.

She stood abruptly, pushing away from the desk. The letter remained.

She moved to the window, pulling back the heavy curtain to gaze at the street below, the first few shards of daylight hitting the cobbles. The neighbourhood was respectable, solidly middle-class, merchants and professionals who'd worked hard for their comforts. Her father had been so proud when they'd moved here from their cramped rooms near the docks.

"Everything we've worked for," he'd said,

sweeping his arm to encompass the modest but elegant house. "Honest work, honest rewards."

She'd done it for the business. For the crew. For the widows and their children.

For him.

But no matter how many reasons she listed, none of them sounded like the truth anymore.

Her thoughts were interrupted by a gentle knock and the soft voice of the maid.

"Will you be taking breakfast in the breakfast room this morning, Miss Warrington?"

"Thank you, Mary, yes, I will. I'll be through shortly," Nell replied, gathering herself from the troubles that had settled over her like dust.

The maid bobbed a curtsy and disappeared down the hall to prepare the morning tray. The scent of freshly baked bread wafted up from the kitchen below, a comforting smell that reminded her of happier times.

Nell glanced down at the letter still in her hand. The familiar curve of her father's handwriting staring back at her. She touched the paper lightly, her voice barely a whisper.

"I'm sorry, Papa," she said to the page, as though her words might somehow reach him across the oceans. "I won't let you down. I promise."

Folding the letter with care, she tucked it beneath the stack of unopened correspondence, then made her way to the breakfast room. She had just settled in with her second cup of tea and was buttering her toast when Mary returned once again, flustered.

"Excuse me, Miss… it's the inspector. He's at the door." The maid's voice dropped to a whisper on the last word, as if merely speaking of the police might summon trouble.

Nell hadn't even heard the bell. Her stomach twisted into a familiar knot, tight and uncomfortable.

What on earth does he want now?

Composing herself, she stood and smoothed her skirts, then glanced in the mirror above the fireplace. She ran her fingers over her hair, adjusting a few pins. Why she cared what the inspector thought of her appearance, she couldn't quite say.

The sound of his boots echoed through the hall, firm and steady, much like the man himself.

"Good morning, Miss Warrington," he said, removing his hat. "Apologies for the intrusion at this early hour."

"It's quite all right, Inspector," she replied, turning to face him with composure. "Please, take a seat."

She gestured toward the chair opposite, then returned to her own. "Can I offer you some tea? Mary has just brought a fresh pot."

"Thank you, no," he said, his tone clipped, his usual business-like manner seemingly restored after their last, more personal encounter.

Nell's stomach sank slightly. She wondered now if she'd imagined the gentle concern she thought she'd seen in him last time. The warmth in his voice when he'd asked after her welfare. Perhaps it had only been wishful thinking.

"Very well," she said. "How can I help you today, Inspector Hart?"

"I'm afraid there's been another fire down at the docks."

Nell's heart lurched. Her teacup froze halfway to her lips.

"No… it can't be possible—" she began, panic rising in her throat.

Hart raised a hand quickly, his expression softening. "No, no, apologies, Miss Warrington. Not your warehouse. It was another shipping company. But it was close to yours. Simmons & Sons, just three buildings down. And the circumstances are… similar." His brow furrowed. "I'm investigating the possibility of a connection."

She exhaled, the relief washing over her in a wave. "That is most unfortunate for them, I mean. But I can't pretend I'm not relieved."

"Of course," he said. "It's only natural."

He paused, his eyes narrowing slightly as he studied her face.

"I have to ask... was there anything unusual you remember about your fire? Anything out of place? I know your workers were clearing up when I visited. Perhaps they uncovered something since?"

Nell's mouth felt suddenly dry. "Not to my knowledge, Inspector," she said, careful to keep her voice steady. "Everything seemed... ordinary, given the circumstances."

Hart reached into his coat pocket and produced a playing card, its edges slightly scorched, its surface streaked with soot.

He laid it face-up on the table between them.

The Jack of Spades stared up at them, his curious profile regarding Nell with knowing eyes.

Nell froze. Her hands, suddenly trembling, slipped beneath the table to hide the reaction.

"This," he said quietly, tapping the card with one finger, "was left at the scene. Not trampled or discarded, but placed deliberately on the warehouse master's desk. Untouched by the flames that consumed everything around it."

He looked at her intently, his gaze searching the depths of her expression for any flicker of recognition.

"It seems we're not merely dealing with sabotage anymore. Someone's leaving a message."

Nell swallowed hard.

"How unusual," she said slowly. "No… I'm afraid I didn't see anything like that at our fire."

Hart didn't respond immediately. His gaze lingered on her face, searching, measuring, weighing the truth of her words against some internal scale of justice. His eyes seemed to see through the carefully constructed walls she'd built around herself.

She held her expression perfectly still.

After a moment, he gave a small nod. And there it was again, that flicker of something gentler in his eyes.

"Very well, Miss Warrington. I trust you," he said, slipping the card back into his pocket. "You're one of the few who's been cooperative in this mess. Most of the other merchants won't even speak to me anymore."

Nell felt the lie rise in her throat like bile.

"I'm just doing my best, Inspector," she said,

hating herself for how easily the words came, how naturally she had stepped into this role of deception. Her father would be ashamed.

He rose from his chair, adjusting his hat under his arm.

"And... I trust everything else is all right?" he added, his voice softer now, pitched for her ears alone though they were the only two in the room. "You've seemed... burdened, of late."

Nell couldn't bear the weight of his concern, of his belief in her. Not when she had just lied to his face

"Quite all right," she said quickly. "Things are… sorting themselves out, to my satisfaction."

"I'm pleased to hear it."

He gave her a final nod, and the briefest smile.

"Well, I won't take up any more of your time, Miss Warrington. If you do remember anything else, anything at all, please send word to the station. I'll come directly."

"Of course."

After he'd gone, Nell sat heavily in her chair. The weight of his trust settled on her chest like a stone.

How has it come to this? she wondered, staring at the empty space on the table where the card had lain.

Lying to the police. In my own home. The house my father worked for with honest hands and honest money.

The tea had grown cold in her cup, a thin film forming on its surface.

You're in too deep now, she told herself. *And sooner or later, these lies will catch up with you. They always do.*

She tapped her fingers on the table, weighing the options she no longer had.

"No need to think," she murmured aloud. "You know what must be done."

She rose with sudden purpose, crossed the hall with quick steps, and pulled her cloak from the hook by the door.

"Mary," she called over her shoulder, "I'm just out on an errand. I'll be back shortly."

"Yes, miss," came the faint reply from the kitchen below.

And with that, she wrapped her cloak tightly around her shoulders and strode out into the cold morning air, her mind set on the right course of action.

The wind had sharpened since morning. Nell pulled her cloak tighter around herself as she made her way through the winding streets of Limehouse. The hem of her skirts caught the occasional puddle, soaking through to her ankles. She barely noticed.

She knew the way to Mei's apothecary by heart now. Left at the faded sign for the chop house, down the alley with the half-broken drainpipe, past the flickering gas lamp that never stayed lit. The path had become almost ritual. Familiar. But today, every step felt heavier than the last.

When she pushed open the apothecary door, the bell above gave a soft chime. The scent of star anise and cloves greeted her, comforting and disorienting all at once.

Mei looked up from the counter where she was bottling tinctures into tiny glass vials, her nimble fingers working with precision.

"Nell," she said, with a tilt of her head. "I wasn't expecting you this early."

"I won't stay long," Nell replied, letting the door fall shut behind her. "I've come to say I'm done."

Mei's hands stilled. "Done?"

"With the shipments. With all of it."

She stepped forward, voice firm. "There was another fire. A playing card left at the scene. Inspector Hart thinks someone's sending a message. He came to me, Mei. Sat in my breakfast room and told me he trusts me." Her voice cracked slightly, but she pressed on. "And I lied to his face."

Mei watched her with the stillness of someone

who had long since stopped reacting to dramatic announcements. Her dark eyes revealed nothing.

"I see."

"No, I don't think you do," Nell snapped, heat rising in her throat. "My father wrote to me. He's proud of me. He thinks I've kept his name clean. Thinks I've done everything right. He still believes in me. And I've dragged that belief through the gutter." Tears welled in her eyes, threatening to spill over onto her flushed cheeks.

Silence hung between them, thick and oppressive.

Mei turned and placed the stoppered vial onto a lacquered tray, arranging it with great precision amongst its companions.

"Your father's ships carry all manner of things, Nell," she said softly. "Do you think every contract he signed was as clean as his conscience?"

"I don't care what he might've ignored," Nell said fiercely. "I'm not going to keep making choices that compromise everything we've worked for. I'm not like you. I can't live with this deception."

Mei finally looked at her then, calm and unflinching. "I never asked you to be like me. But I did expect you to understand the stakes."

"I do," Nell said. "That's precisely why I'm stopping now."

Mei gave a small, almost imperceptible sigh, and turned away.

"The next shipment is already en route," she said flatly.

Nell blinked. "What?"

"It left three days ago from Canton. It's aboard the *Lotus Pearl*. Arriving in under a fortnight."

"But… you said—"

"I said one shipment at first. Then I said another. And now I'm telling you this one is already in motion. You think you're the only one who's committed something here? That you alone bear the weight of consequence?"

Nell's fists clenched at her sides. "You should've told me."

"You should've made up your mind sooner," Mei replied smoothly. "The gears are turning. If they stop now, they'll crush more than just you. There are dockhands expecting coin. Families relying on what they think is coming. If you disappear now, someone else will pay the price."

Nell took a shaky breath, her voice quieter now. "I never meant for this to go so far."

Mei's expression softened a fraction. "No one ever does."

A long silence stretched between them. Only the quiet bubbling of something brewing on the back stove filled the space.

Finally, Nell said, "This is the last one."

Mei nodded. "Of course it is."

But her tone made it sound like she'd heard that before.

Nell turned and walked out into the cold, her footsteps as heavy as her heart. As heavy as the disappointment she knew she would see in her father's eyes should the truth ever come to light.

CHAPTER 8

The clock had just chimed four when the knock came.

Nell looked up from her desk, where she'd been staring blankly at the same line in the ledger for the better part of an hour. The figures no longer made sense. Or perhaps she simply no longer cared to understand them.

The knock came again, causing her to remember that it was Mary's day off. The house felt unnaturally quiet without the maid's soft footfalls and gentle humming.

She snapped the ledgers shut, and left her study, smoothing her skirts as she went. She opened the door to find Inspector Hart standing on the threshold, his hat in one hand, coat damp from the drizzle outside.

"Miss Warrington," he said with a small nod. "Apologies for dropping by unannounced. Again."

Nell's heart sank, but she smiled politely. "Of course, Inspector. Please, come in."

She led him back to the drawing room, where the fire had been stoked into a respectable glow, and gestured to the chair opposite hers. He sat with a stiffness that suggested he wasn't planning to stay long. His eyes, however, lingered on the room's details, taking in everything with the careful scrutiny that had earned him his reputation.

"I'll not take up too much of your time," he said. "Just a few follow-up questions. There's been some development with the fires."

Nell prayed the flush creeping up her neck wouldn't betray her. "A development?"

Hart nodded. "We've reason to believe these incidents may be coordinated. There's been another blaze down in Poplar. Similar pattern. And we're receiving word of... interference in cargo flow. Delays. Bribes. Intimidation."

Nell kept her expression neutral. "What does that have to do with me?"

"Likely nothing," he said quickly, though his eyes never left her face. "But in light of all this, customs has issued a temporary clampdown. Effective immediately. All inbound cargo over the next forty-eight hours will be subject to full inspection. No exceptions."

Nell's breath caught, only for a second. She hoped he didn't notice.

"We're urging all businesses to be prepared," Hart went on. "I thought it best you heard it from me rather than an irate customs officer."

"That's very kind of you," she said, managing a tight smile. "I'll notify my staff."

Hart leaned back, studying her. "You always seem to be ahead of things."

Nell blinked. "Not always."

There was a pause. His gaze drifted to the fireplace, then back to her. "May I ask—how are things? You've had a rough few weeks."

Nell hesitated. The room felt suddenly warmer. Closer.

"I'm managing," she said at last. "There's always something."

His expression softened. "That's what worries me."

The words struck deeper than he likely intended.

She rose abruptly, forcing a smile. "I'll walk you to the door."

He stood, slipping on his hat. "As I said—if there's anything else. Anything unusual. Don't hesitate to send word."

"I won't."

He paused at the threshold. Rain pattered softly beyond, forming puddles on the cobblestones. "I meant what I said before, Nell. I trust you."

And then he was gone, vanishing into the rain like a man who had just handed her a live fuse without knowing it.

Nell closed the door slowly. She leaned her forehead against the polished wood, eyes closed.

Forty-eight hours.

The *Lotus Pearl* was due in less than twelve.

The grandfather clock in the hall continued its relentless ticking, counting down to a disaster she could neither prevent nor escape. With no time to think, she grabbed her cloak and headed out the door, hailing a cab.

By the time Nell reached the Chinese quarter, the panic rising in her chest had become unbearable. The winding lanes, still shadowed in the grey wash of late afternoon, seemed narrower than usual, pressing in on her from all sides. Shopfronts glowed dimly through the mist, their signs painted in gold brushstrokes she couldn't read.

She reached the apothecary and didn't bother knocking. The bell above the door chimed sharply as she entered, breath ragged, heart still hammering from the ride and the fear that had chased her the entire way.

Mei looked up from a stack of tiny parchment-wrapped bundles, her movements as serene as ever.

"You're early," she said.

"We have a problem." Nell crossed the shop floor in quick strides, her voice tight. "A serious one."

Mei didn't flinch. "Tea?"

"No, I—God, do you ever panic?"

"Rarely," Mei replied, turning to pour from a waiting pot anyway. "Sit. You're wet."

"I don't care," Nell snapped. "The Inspector came to see me. He warned me—there's a full customs clampdown for the next two days. Every shipment coming in will be searched. Thoroughly. The *Lotus Pearl* arrives tomorrow morning. Do you understand what that means?"

Mei placed a steaming cup of tea on the counter between them. "It means we must be precise."

"Precise?" Nell nearly laughed. "It means we'll be caught. You, me, everyone. Elijah thinks I'm—" She broke off, biting the inside of her cheek. "He *trusts* me, Mei."

"And that bothers you," Mei said, gently.

"It should."

Mei's expression remained impassive, but she moved with quiet efficiency, untying a parcel of waxed cloth and extracting a small, rolled document. She wrote a short message in tight, deliberate strokes, then sealed it with a plain black cord.

From the back of the shop, she called out something in Cantonese. A few seconds later, a boy of about twelve emerged from the curtained doorway, barefoot and alert. Mei handed him the scroll and said something quickly in a low, commanding voice.

The boy nodded once, then bolted out the front door without a word.

Nell watched him vanish into the mist. "What did you tell him?"

"To inform our man at the dock," Mei replied. "The crates will be marked differently. They'll be pulled early, before the officers begin their sweep. He knows how to handle the porters."

"That's it?" Nell asked, blinking. "A message and a child?"

Mei turned back to her calmly. "Speed matters

LILY BOURNE

more than muscle in situations like this. He'll be there in half the time it would take anyone else."

Nell sat down heavily on the nearest stool, head in her hands. "We're going to be caught."

"No," Mei said. "We're going to survive."

"You sound so sure."

Mei tilted her head. "Because I've been here before."

A long silence settled between them. The only sound was the soft drip of rain outside, and the tick of the apothecary's narrow wall clock.

"I don't want to do this anymore," Nell whispered.

Mei set the teapot aside and crossed the room, kneeling beside her gracefully.

"Then don't," she said. "But you'll still have to deal with the storm you've already called down."

Nell didn't answer. Her fingers were laced tightly in her lap, knuckles pale.

"You're thinking of him," Mei added softly.

Nell looked up. "What?"

"The inspector," Mei said. "Elijah Hart. I can see you're trying not to care how he sees you."

"I don't care how he sees me," Nell said quickly. Too quickly.

Mei raised one eyebrow. "So it doesn't matter

that he trusts you? That he sits in your parlour and tells you you're different? You're clean. You're *better*."

"I just don't want him to realise he's put his faith in the wrong person."

"That's not what I asked."

Nell stood abruptly. Her stool scraped against the wooden floor. "This has nothing to do with him."

Mei remained where she was, unmoved. "It has everything to do with him. Or at least with how you want to be seen by him. You're building a version of yourself he'll never recognise."

Nell turned her back, pacing to the window. "You think I'm playing games?"

"No," Mei said. "I think it's dangerous."

That landed heavier than any accusation.

After a moment, Mei spoke again, gentler this time. "It's not a weakness, you know. Wanting someone to see the best in you. But it becomes one if you start lying to yourself in the process."

Nell didn't respond. Couldn't. Her chest felt too tight to speak.

Outside, footsteps splashed through puddles. The street hummed with life again.

From the front door, the bell jingled softly. Another customer.

Mei stood, aware that the conversation was

going nowhere. "The shipment will be handled," she said. "Now, go home. Dry off. You'll need your wits tomorrow."

Nell lingered for one heartbeat longer, then nodded and made her way to the door.

As she stepped out into the street, the rain falling light but steady around her, she didn't know whether it was fear, guilt, or something else entirely, curling low in her stomach.

The next morning dawned as grey as Nell's mood as she made her way through the docks toward the shipping company office.

Ordinarily, this early hour brought with it a slow, sleepy stirring of life. The rhythmic clatter of crates, the murmur of voices, the creak of mooring ropes as ships gently nudged against the quay. But today, the docks buzzed with unfamiliar energy.

Uniformed customs officers were stationed at nearly every berth, their presence unmistakable. Harbour patrol boats drifted along the Thames like watchful eyes on the water. The usual quiet shuffle had been replaced by the bark of orders, the snap of inspection papers, and the heavy footfalls of officials demanding to see manifests and bills of lading.

Inside the office, Nell lit the little stove and set the kettle on to boil, hoping for five minutes' peace with a cup of tea, to steady her jangling nerves and brace herself for what lay ahead. She could only hope Mei's message had found its intended recipient, and that arrangements were in place to ensure the special crates were unloaded without incident.

She had just poured the steaming water into her teacup when a dockhand opened the door.

"If you please, miss—the *Lotus Pearl* is pulling up now. Thought you might want to know, what with all these officials about."

Nell looked up, masking the agitation that flared in her chest.

"Thank you," she said calmly. "I'll be out shortly."

Once the door was closed again, she took a deep breath and carefully arranged her features into something resembling composure, despite the churning panic inside.

Stepping outside, she saw the *Lotus Pearl* draw up to the dock, the gangplank lowered and fastened with speed. As she approached, a customs officer turned toward her.

"You must be Miss Warrington?"

"That's correct," she replied. "Is there anything I can do to help?"

"No need, miss. I've already received the manifest from your foreman. We'll be checking every crate that comes off the ship. But if you'd care to remain on hand for any questions, that would be helpful."

"Of course," she said with a polite smile that barely reached her eyes. "Anything I can do to ensure the shipment proceeds smoothly."

She stepped back, arms folded tightly across her chest, her hands buried in her cloak to stop them trembling. Crate after crate was wheeled down the gangplank, and now she spotted them. The ones marked with the discreet symbol she knew all too well. The ones that mattered.

Her heart pounded as she watched one of the officers lift a crate and inspect the label. He paused, squinting, then checked the manifest again, twice.

"Is there a problem, Officer?" she asked, keeping her voice calm.

"It's just… I don't recognise this mark here," he said, tapping the crate's corner.

Nell stepped forward to get a better look when a sudden, thunderous bang echoed from behind a stack of cargo.

The dock erupted into chaos.

Men dived for cover as a stack of crates exploded in splinters. Barrels from another ship went tumbling, their contents scattering across the ground. A thick smoke wafted into the air, and shouts erupted in every direction.

"I say, what's going on over there?" barked the officer, straining to hear over the din.

"Looks like a cart's overturned!" another man shouted. "Could be some explosives—maybe blasting powder in one of the shipments!"

The officer swore under his breath. "What next?"

Turning back to Nell, he grimaced. "I'm terribly sorry, Miss Warrington, but I need to help sort this out."

She could hardly believe her luck. A breath of pure, dizzying relief passed through her.

"Of course, Officer," she said quickly. "You're needed. Please, go. I'll finish up here. I have the manifest."

He hesitated only a moment before handing it to her. "Thank you, Miss Warrington," he said, and turned to dash into the commotion.

As he disappeared into the crowd, Nell's eyes scanned the chaos. And then she saw him.

Across the yard, leaning against a stack of crates as if nothing unusual had happened, stood a figure far too relaxed for the situation. Flicking a coin and grinning with unmistakable smugness.

Jonny Collins.

She narrowed her eyes, catching his gaze. He gave a low chuckle and winked at her.

Was that you? she mouthed silently.

He raised one brow and gave a small salute before melting back into the shadows behind the crates.

The inspection abandoned, Nell hurriedly signed off the remaining crates and saw them wheeled away, each one disappearing into the warehouse helping to calm her heart that was still hammering behind her ribs.

After a steadying cup of tea in the office - no one would know she'd added a tot of brandy - she made her way into the warehouse, keen to get the crates ready and on the way to their next destination.

As she surveyed the crates, she heard whistling coming from the alley behind. Suspecting a worker shirking his duties, and in no mood to have attention drawn to the warehouse, she strode out to confront him.

And there he stood, the very picture of ease. Coat unbuttoned, sleeves rolled, one boot braced against the wall like he hadn't just orchestrated a minor dockyard explosion.

"You've got a nerve," she said, stepping into view.

Jonny looked up, the coin still dancing across his knuckles. "Hello to you too, sweetheart."

"Don't call me that."

"Noted," he said, slipping the coin into his pocket. "Though you seemed rather fond of me when those officers turned tail."

Nell folded her arms. "Fond isn't the word I'd use."

"Oh?" He pushed off the wall and took a few lazy steps toward her. "Then what would you call it? Eternal gratitude? Begrudging admiration? Secret longing?"

"You're insufferable."

"And yet here you are."

He was close to her now. The scent of tobacco clung to him, mixed with salt and smoke. His smirk was infuriating. His proximity more so. She could see the stubble along his jawline and a small scar near his right temple that she'd never noticed before.

"You could've gotten someone hurt," she snapped, tilting her chin up. "You didn't think that through."

"I thought it through very carefully," he said. "Two barrels, half full of sand, one handful of powder to make a bang. Flash, noise, drama—no damage. You're welcome."

She narrowed her eyes. "You took an unnecessary risk."

"And saved your pretty neck doing it."

The smile faded just slightly from his lips, replaced by something quieter. "You were going to get caught, Nell. You were seconds away from losing everything."

"I didn't ask you to save me."

"No. But you needed it."

There was a beat of silence. His gaze held hers. He wasn't teasing anymore. The usual mischief in his eyes had given way to something more sincere, more disarming.

"You and me," he said, voice low. "We make a good team."

"I'm not part of your team," she said quickly.

"Funny. You say that, but you let me clean up your mess. Again."

"I wouldn't call it a mess. I'd call it a very tightly-run operation that you barged into with a box of tricks and a flair for dramatics."

Jonny threw his head back and laughed. "God, I do love that mouth of yours."

"I swear to God, if you—"

He held up his hands in surrender, though his grin was still very much in place.

He looked away for a moment and his expression turned thoughtful, quieter. The sort of expression people wore when remembering something they didn't want to.

"My brother used to say I couldn't go two days without stirring trouble," he said, almost to himself.

Nell blinked. "You have a brother?"

"Had." His jaw tensed slightly. "He was the golden one. Always did things right. Kept the family name clean. I just made sure we ate."

There was something in the way he said it, not defensive, not boastful. Just matter-of-fact. Like he didn't expect sympathy. Like he'd long stopped hoping for any.

Nell's breath caught.

"You don't talk about him," she said, curious despite herself.

Jonny shrugged. "No one asks."

More silence stretched between them, as Nell felt something in her chest. Something tentative and traitorous. A warmth she hadn't expected and didn't welcome.

He turned back to her, features snapped back into place, the grin returning. "You don't have to like me, Nell," he said. "You just have to admit we're useful to each other."

"And what? Ride this out together until we end up swinging from the gallows?"

He shrugged. "There are worse ways to go."

She shook her head, but the laugh slipped out before she could stop it, utterly against her will. Jonny's grin widened, this time without mockery.

"Now there's that smile," he said. "Almost makes me believe you're not completely immune to me."

"I am."

"Sure you are."

He turned then, as if that was that, and strolled back toward the street.

Just before he disappeared, he glanced over his shoulder. "You need me, Nell. And I'll be around. Sooner or later, you'll stop pretending you don't want me around."

And with that, he was gone.

Nell stood rooted to the spot, cheeks burning with rage, or could it be desire?

She pressed her back to the warehouse wall, staring up at the grey sky above, still catching its breath after the storm.

She wasn't sure which scared her more—

That he was right.

Or that part of her didn't want him to be wrong.

CHAPTER 9

The docks after dark were a different world, quieter, softer, bathed in the glow of the gas lamps flickering along the quay. The Thames lapped against the pilings, and the usual shouts of the labourers had long faded into the night air.

Nell wasn't sure why she'd gone for a walk instead of heading home. Perhaps she was chasing the cool air, or the silence. The hem of her cloak dragged slightly across the damp boards as she wandered, seemingly aimless but drawn inexorably forward.

She found Jonny leaning against a stack of crates near the water's edge, arms folded, coat collar turned up against the breeze. He looked like he'd been waiting for her, though she hadn't said she'd be coming.

"How do you always know where I'll be?" she asked.

"I don't," he said, pushing off the crate with a grin. "I just assume you'll come looking for me eventually."

She rolled her eyes, but there was a hint of a smile. "You're impossible."

"And yet," he said, taking a step closer, "you're still talking to me."

He reached into his coat pocket and pulled out a small flask. "Drink?"

Nell hesitated only a moment before taking it. She took a swig—brandy. Strong. Smooth. It warmed her from within, chasing away the evening chill.

"Thought you needed to let your hair down," Jonny said. "You've looked like a woman on the edge of implosion all week."

"Charming," she muttered, handing the flask back. Their fingers brushed, a fleeting contact that caused her breath to quicken.

They walked together along the edge of the dock, the boards creaking softly underfoot. For a while, they said nothing, content to exist in the rare peaceful moment. Then Jonny began telling her a story. Something about a failed heist involving a crate of fake cognac, a belligerent goat, and a tailor who had to flee the city dressed as a nun.

Nell laughed so hard she nearly doubled over.

"Stop it," she gasped. "I can't breathe."

"It's all true," he said, feigning wounded pride. "Except maybe the goat. But the tailor really *was* a nun for three days. Took to it surprisingly well."

She wiped her eyes. "I hate that you make me laugh."

"Yes," he said softly, "but you needed it."

She looked at him then, properly. His grin had faded just enough. His eyes were dark in the gaslight, unreadable. The night hummed around them, still and waiting.

Jonny took a step closer. He reached up and tucked a stray strand of hair behind her ear. His hand lingered, warm against her skin. She didn't pull away.

"Nell," he said, voice low, "I know I'm trouble. But you—"

She didn't let him finish.

She reached up and kissed him.

It was instinctive and reckless and everything she wasn't supposed to do. His hands found her waist as hers slid into his hair, the kiss deepening with a hunger that surprised even her. He tasted like brandy, like something wild and wrong and liberating.

When she finally pulled back, breathless, his forehead rested against hers.

"Well," he said, voice rough, "that wasn't very businesslike."

"Neither are you," she replied.

He chuckled softly. "We could leave right now. Hop a barge to nowhere."

She smiled, but there was a fear behind it. "You'd hate nowhere."

"Not with you in it."

The moment lingered, thick with possibility, with temptation. A ship's bell rang in the distance, as if marking the significance of the choice before her.

Then Nell stepped back, gently but firmly. "I can't."

"Not yet," he said.

She didn't reply.

He didn't push her.

Instead, he took her hand for one quiet second, rough fingers brushing her palm, then turned and disappeared into the shadows, leaving her on the dock, heart hammering like she'd just jumped from something very high and survived the fall.

The next day, Nell rose early, though she hadn't slept. She'd tossed beneath the blankets, her skin still tingling from the heat of Jonny's kiss, her mind playing and replaying every word, every look, every reckless moment.

The rain had passed in the night, leaving the sky pale and clear, the river glassy and deceptive in its calm. She brewed tea in the shipping office kitchen and took it to the window that overlooked the eastern moorings.

Everything looked so... normal. As if the night before hadn't happened.

But something had shifted. In her.

She'd let herself be seen. Not as the responsible daughter, not as the competent businesswoman. Just as Nell. She wasn't sure whether she felt free or sick.

Jonny made her feel alive. Like she could burn the rulebook and rewrite it in her own hand. But Elijah.

She closed her eyes.

Elijah made her want to *be* good. Better. Like the girl her father believed in. The one she wasn't entirely sure existed anymore. Her fingers traced the cool glass of the window, as if trying to connect with something solid and real amidst her swirling thoughts.

Her gaze drifted down to the warehouse floor, where men were already beginning to unload the next round of goods. Everything looked in order. Everything was running on time.

So why did she feel like she was seconds from losing control? She felt as though she could stand at that window thinking it through all day and still not come up with the answers. The certainty she'd once prided herself on seemed to have dissolved overnight.

She didn't hear him arrive.

When she turned from the window, Elijah Hart was standing in the open doorway of the office, his hat in his hands, his expression unreadable.

"Inspector," she said, startled. "I wasn't expecting visitors this early."

"I thought I'd take my walk by the river," he said mildly. "Seemed as good a place as any to start the morning."

She gestured vaguely. "Would you like some tea?"

He stepped inside but didn't sit. "No, thank you. This won't take long."

Nell's spine straightened. "Is something wrong?"

"I heard you've been making payments to the

families of the *Eleanor* crew," he said evenly. "Quite generous sums, from what I understand."

Nell hesitated. "They needed help. Their husbands were loyal workers. It felt like the right thing to do."

"I'm not disagreeing," he said. "But it's my understanding that the insurance claim hasn't been cleared yet."

"I... found some funds," she said, reaching for the lie she'd rehearsed. "An old investment account of my father's. I remembered it when I was going through the ledgers."

She hated how easy it was to sound calm. How the lies now slipped from her tongue with such ease.

Elijah's brow furrowed slightly. He didn't speak.

Eventually, he said, "That's convenient."

"I suppose it is."

There was a long silence. The ticking of the clock on the wall seemed to grow unnaturally loud.

"Nell," he said finally, voice quieter, "you don't have to lie to me."

Her fingers tightened around her teacup. "I'm not."

He nodded slowly, as if pretending to believe her cost more than he was willing to admit. "All right."

He turned as though to leave, then paused in the doorway. "One more thing."

She looked up sharply.

"There's talk on the docks," he said. "Your name… linked with certain company."

Nell's blood ran cold.

"Undesirables," he added. "Men who wouldn't hesitate to bring you down with them."

She drew herself up. "My personal life is no concern of yours, Inspector."

He turned back to her then, meeting her eyes. And when he spoke again, it was no longer with the voice of a policeman.

"It is, actually. When it puts you in danger."

That struck deeper than she expected. She didn't have an answer for it. His concern, genuine and unguarded, made her deception feel all the more shameful.

"I thought I knew who you were," he said softly. "But lately… I'm not so sure."

Nell's voice was cold. "Then maybe you never did."

The look on his face was unreadable—part hurt, part disbelief, part something else she didn't want to name.

He gave her a final nod, then stepped out and was

gone. His footsteps echoed down the wooden stairs, each one a painful reminder of the distance growing between them.

She stood very still for a long moment. The tea had gone cold in her hand.

He hadn't said Jonny's name. But he hadn't needed to.

And the worst part?

He was right to be worried.

Nell stood rooted in place, her arms folded tight across her chest, as though she could hold herself together with sheer will alone. The morning light filtering through the windows seemed too harsh now, illuminating truths she preferred to keep in shadow.

Elijah's words echoed in the quiet:

"I thought I knew who you were." "It puts you in danger." "You don't have to lie to me."

Her jaw clenched, shame crawling up her neck. She hadn't wanted to lie. Not to him. Not when he'd looked at her like that, with eyes that still searched for the woman he believed her to be.

Not when he trusted her.

She turned slowly, facing the window again, the tea cooling untouched beside her. The docks bustled below—men moving goods, shouting orders, laughing in the morning sun. Life went on, indifferent to her private storm. Ships continued to arrive and depart, tides ebbed and flowed, all with a certainty she no longer possessed.

She pressed her fingers to the glass, watching a cargo ship cut through the river's surface like a blade. It reminded her of Johnny—fast, dangerous, slicing through everything in his path with swagger and a grin. Unapologetic in his chaos.

He made her feel alive. Uncaged. Like the weight she'd carried alone for so long didn't have to be hers forever. In his presence, she glimpsed a version of herself free of expectation, wild and free and answering to no one.

But Elijah…

He made her want to be worthy of that trust. To be the woman her father believed in. The one who wrote letters with promises she was now breaking, line by line. With Elijah, she remembered the girl she'd once been, principled, certain, her moral compass unwavering.

Johnny made her forget the rules.

Elijah made her remember why they mattered.

She turned from the window and sat at her desk, her shoulders sagging beneath the invisible burden she carried. Her gaze fell to the stack of unopened letters from creditors, contracts she hadn't dared sign, and the thick envelope still tucked in the drawer—Mei's cash. Clean in its presentation. Filthy in every other sense.

For a long moment, she simply stared at the chaos of her carefully managed world. The dual lives. The masks. The fire she'd lit and now didn't know how to put out. How quickly it had all unravelled, like loose thread that, when pulled, revealed the fragility of everything she'd built.

She reached for her father's letter and traced his familiar script with her fingertip, as though the contact might summon his wisdom when she needed it most.

"You're stronger than you think."

She closed her eyes, the weight of it all pressing down on her chest. The lingering scent of Johnny's tobacco still clung to her skin, while Elijah's disappointment hung heavy in the air around her.

"I don't feel strong," she whispered.

She wasn't sure if she was speaking to her father, Elijah, Johnny—or herself. The words dissolved into the silence, unanswered.

Outside, the warehouse bell rang, summoning the next round of labour. Another shipment. Another day pretending she had it under control.

The sound jarred her back to the present, to responsibilities that wouldn't wait for her heart to find its bearings.

Nell rose and straightened her shoulders. She smoothed her skirts with trembling hands that soon steadied. She tucked away her father's letter and closed the drawer on Mei's money. The mask of competence slipped back into place.

She wasn't ready to choose.

Not between men. Not between right and wrong. Not yet.

But she knew the time was coming. And fast.

Each tide brought it closer, each decision narrowed her path. The crossroads loomed before her, unavoidable and demanding. Soon she would have to step in one direction or another, and there would be no turning back.

And when that moment came someone was going to get hurt.

CHAPTER 10

The knock at the office door was soft, almost apologetic.

Nell looked up from the ledger she wasn't truly reading, a frown creasing her brow. Visitors weren't usual at this hour—not unless something had gone wrong at the docks. The shipping tallies had blurred before her eyes, numbers swimming together as her mind wandered elsewhere.

"Come in," she called, setting her pen aside.

The door opened hesitantly, and Mary, the housemaid, stepped inside. She looked out of place amid the cluttered ledgers and battered crates—her sensible bonnet damp from the river mist, her gloved hands twisting nervously. She stood half in shadow, as if reluctant to deliver whatever had brought her here.

Nell's stomach dipped.

"Mary? What is it? Has something happened at the house?"

Mary shook her head quickly. "No, miss. Nothing there. It's just… this came. From overseas." She stepped forward, offering a small, cream-coloured envelope. The corners were battered from the long journey. The black wax seal smudged, but unmistakable.

Nell took it without a word. Her fingers trembled slightly.

Mary hesitated, as if reluctant to leave her alone, but Nell managed a small smile. "Thank you. Please, go and get warm. I'll be along shortly."

With a worried look, Mary bobbed a curtsey and backed out of the room.

Nell stared at the letter for a long moment before sliding her thumb under the seal. She noted the date stamped upon it, nearly two months old. News travelled slowly from the East.

The paper inside was thin and brittle with travel. She unfolded it carefully.

The letter was short. Official. Blunt.

It is with regret that we inform you of the death of Mr.

Henry Warrington, who succumbed to fever on the 17th of June, while stationed in Calcutta. All personal effects to be forwarded upon receipt of instructions. Our condolences on your loss.

No flourish. No sentiment. No final words.

Nell read it twice, three times, the words refusing to settle properly in her mind. The neat handwriting of some clerk who had never met her father, never heard his laugh, never seen his eyes crinkle when he smiled.

Dead.

The man who had built everything, who had worked the docks with his bare hands, who had saved for her schoolbooks and sat proudly at her mother's graveside. Gone. Without warning. Without even a chance to write one last letter home. Without knowing what she had become in his absence.

The room tilted slightly. She sat down hard in the chair behind her desk, the letter crumpling in her hand.

Her father was dead.

There would be no triumphant return, no new contracts, no debts miraculously paid. Only this: a handful of unpaid bills, a mountain of expectations, and the sudden, crushing realisation that she was alone.

Truly, irrevocably alone.

A sharp knock at the warehouse gates outside jolted her. Dockhands shouting. Crates being loaded. The world continued on, indifferent to the hollowed-out space growing inside her chest. From her window, she could see men laughing, arguing, carrying on with their day as if nothing had changed.

She closed her eyes briefly, gathering herself.

No tears. Not here. Not now.

When she opened them again, her gaze hardened.

The business was hers now. Every debt. Every responsibility. Every risk.

And if she had to barter with devils to keep it standing, then so be it. Neither Johnny nor Elijah nor anyone else would dictate her path forward. Her father's legacy, complicated as it might be, was now solely in her hands.

Nell folded the letter carefully, smoothing the creases with steady hands, and tucked it into the inside pocket of her coat, close to her heart, where no one could see the weakness it carried.

There would be time for mourning later.

For now, there was only survival.

She picked up her pen once more, dipped it in ink, and returned to the ledger. The figures no longer swam before her eyes. Each number was sharp, clear, demanding her attention. Her father had taught her that accounts never lied. They told the story of what was, not what one wished to be true.

And the story they told now was one of precarious balance, of a business teetering on the edge.

Nell returned to the Islington house that evening long after the sun had dipped below the rooftops, casting the street into a hushed silence.

The hallway greeted her with darkness, save for the faint glow of the gaslight near the stairs, its flame dancing in the draft. She passed Mary in the corridor, the housekeeper's face etched with concern.

"There's some lamb broth kept warm, Miss Eleanor. You've not eaten since—"

"Thank you, Mary. Perhaps later." said Nell as she continued toward her father's study, her steps measured despite the heaviness in her chest.

The room stood as a memorial to its former occupant, untouched. It smelled faintly of pipe tobacco and old paper. She hadn't been in here for weeks, not properly. She'd merely peeked in, sometimes standing at the threshold as if waiting for permission to enter a space that now, by all rights, belonged to her. She'd left most of the household finances untouched, convincing herself there would be time to sort it all when he returned.

Now there would be no return. The telegram with its blunt message—"Regret to inform... complications of fever... sincere condolences..."—had seen to that.

She closed the door behind her and lit the oil lamp on the desk. She sat in her father's chair and ran her hand over the green blotter worn smooth at the corners. The brass key to his drawer hung from the ring at her waist—he'd entrusted it to her before his departure, "just in case."

The lock turned with a click. Inside: ledgers bound in cloth, receipts carefully arranged by date, thin folders tied with twine that had grown brittle with age. And there, beneath it all, the last will and testament she'd helped him draft before his journey to India, barely glanced at since.

"I'll be back before you need to worry about any of this, Nell," he'd said with confidence, the same tone he'd used when assuring her that her mother would recover, all those years ago. She should have known better than to believe him twice.

She started with the ledgers, her fingers tracing the neat columns of her father's handwriting. The truth unfolded with merciless speed and hideous clarity.

Her father, the great merchant venturer, paragon of commercial wisdom, had been keeping the business afloat on a patchwork of credit lines and short-term loans. A catastrophic investment in a coastal shipping venture that had literally sunk with three vessels in a November storm. Two large debts with prominent lenders. Hawkins and Sons to the tune of £2,000, and Lord Carrington's private bank for nearly twice that sum, both now transferred to her name with her father's passing.

She dropped the ledger onto the desk, her fingers pressed against her forehead where a dull ache had begun to throb.

No savings. No contingency. No inherited wisdom to guide her through this labyrinth of financial ruin. Just an avalanche of numbers and no one left to hold it back.

She stood abruptly, the chair scraping against the floorboards as she began pacing the room. The walls, once lined with maps of far-off trading routes and leather-bound books on commerce and navigation, now seemed to close in on her, the ceiling pressing down with the weight of expectations she couldn't possibly fulfill.

She'd promised him. Promised to protect the legacy he'd worked so hard to build.

But this storm... this wasn't a squall to be weathered with grit and determination. This was a deluge that threatened to sweep away everything—the house, the business, their good name in London society.

Her fingers traced the spines of his books absently. "The Modern Merchant's Guide." "Principles of International Trade." "Ethics and Commerce." She nearly laughed at the last one. What good had ethics done her father in the end? What good would they do her now?

The clock chimed eleven, each note resonating in the quiet room. Decisions couldn't wait for morning light or clearer heads. Creditors rarely extended such courtesies, especially to women trying to navigate a man's world alone.

She returned to the desk, pulled a clean sheet of her father's expensive stationery, one of the few luxuries remaining and began drafting a letter to Mei Ling.

Not flowery. Not polite. Not the carefully

composed correspondence of a gentleman's daughter.

Just one line, written in a hand steadier than it had any right to be:

"I'm ready for more."

She folded it with care, sealing it with wax but no family crest. An envelope with no name, it didn't need one. Mei's people would know who it came from.

Her grief had nowhere to go. Her sorrow had no one left to hear it. Her future had no certain path.

But her debts had very real ears. Her creditors had very real demands. And London's underworld had very real opportunities for a woman with nothing left to lose.

She extinguished the lamp and sat in darkness, the outline of the city visible through the study window. Somewhere out there were the answers to her predicament, answers her father would never have contemplated, much less condoned.

She was done pretending there was another way out. Done being the dutiful daughter waiting for rescue.

Later that evening, against her better judgement, Nell found herself pushing open the tavern door. It wasn't quite the dive Nell expected—it was worse. Cracked glass in the windows, a fire that barely smoked, the stink of beer and sweat clinging to the walls. The kind of place where men traded more than money and asked fewer questions than answers.

She hesitated in the doorway just long enough to scan the room. Her presence drew a few lingering glances—a woman alone, and clearly out of place despite her deliberately plain attire. Two sailors nudged each other by the bar. A grey-haired man with a scar splitting his lip raised his tankard in mock salute. Then she saw him.

Jonny Collins was at the back, lounging like a prince among pirates. Coat slung over the chair beside him, a drink in hand, his shirt collar open just enough to suggest the day's proper conventions had long been abandoned. His smile turned lazy and unmistakably smug the moment their eyes met.

He stood as she approached, a flicker of warmth in his eyes.

"Evening, partner," he said, voice low and full of that swaggering charm. "Didn't think you'd come."

"You asked me to," Nell replied, brushing past him as she sat. "I'm not in the habit of playing games."

Jonny slid back into his seat, gesturing to the

drink already poured and waiting for her. Not the watered-down gin the other patrons nursed, but something amber and expensive. He'd expected her, despite his words.

"I'm not either," he said. "Though the last time I saw you, I seem to recall you started one."

Nell's stomach flipped. The kiss. She'd barely let herself think about it since, let alone what it meant or why, of all people to turn to in a moment of weakness, she'd chosen him. But clearly, he had thought about it. Often.

"I was upset," she said quickly, fingers curling around the glass without drinking. "Things have been, difficult."

His gaze softened, the cockiness ebbing away to something that looked like concern. "I know. I heard about your father."

She tensed, eyes darting to his face. "From who?"

He shrugged. "People talk. I listen."

For a moment, neither of them said anything. Then Jonny leaned forward, forearms resting on the table, voice dropping to something only she could hear. "Look, I'm not here to push. You've had a week. But I wanted you to know, you've got options, Nell. You don't have to carry this alone."

She met his eyes, searching for the ulterior

motive she was certain must lurk there. No one offered help without expecting something in return. Especially not men like Jonny Collins, whose connections ran far deeper into the city's shadows than he ever admitted.

She met his eyes. "You think smuggling opium is going to take the weight off my shoulders?"

"I think it already has," he said, not unkindly. "You're still standing. That says something."

She hated that he wasn't wrong.

Jonny reached into his coat and laid out a small folded document—something like a contract, but coded and vague. No names, just quantities and initials.

"This is the next level," he said. "Regular shipments. Safe routes. You're protected."

"Protected by who?"

He leaned back, watching her with that unnerving intensity that made her feel like he was memorising the contours of her face. "People who make sure the right crates get waved through customs without inspection. People who don't like surprises or attention from the wrong quarters. People who own shares in businesses you'd be shocked to learn about." He paused, letting the implications sink in. "But they see you as an asset, Nell. And they don't offer second chances."

She stared at the document. On paper, it was nothing. Meaningless without context. In reality, it was everything: financial salvation, social damnation, criminal conspiracy.

"And what do *you* see me as?" she asked, forcing herself to meet his gaze.

Jonny didn't smile this time.

"I see a woman with steel in her spine, bleeding herself dry to protect a business no one else would've saved," he said quietly. "I see someone who kissed me like she meant it, and then ran. I see intelligence being wasted on men who don't deserve it." He reached for his drink but didn't take his eyes off her. "And I see someone afraid to admit she's good at this. This game you claim not to play."

Her throat tightened, words suddenly difficult to form. "You think that kiss meant I've chosen you?"

"Over Hart, you mean?" His eyebrow raised as she blushed.

He shrugged. "You don't have to choose me. Just don't pretend we're not a good team."

"I'm not sure we are," she whispered, more to herself than to him. "A team, I mean."

"You kissed me, Nell. Not Hart. Me." The words

hung between them, charged with everything they weren't saying. "In your darkest moment, you came to me.

She stood suddenly, unable to sit still any longer.

"I need time," she said. "To think. To breathe."

"Take it," Jonny said, rising too, leaving money on the table that would more than cover their bill. "But don't wait too long. The river doesn't stop because you're grieving. Neither do your creditors."

He didn't touch her this time.

He just looked at her like he already knew which way she'd go.

And it scared her how much of her wanted him to be right.

She strolled back to the docks, not wanting to be at the house, with every corner reminding her of her father. The dockhands had gone home hours ago, leaving her to the quiet scratch of pen on paper and the distant cries of gulls wheeling over the Thames. This was where she felt most at peace now, among the practical workings of the business, where grief had to wait its turn.

It was late when she was disturbed by a knock at the office door, quieter than usual. Three soft raps, hesitant, almost apologetic.

Nell looked up from the ledger, her hand frozen

mid-calculation. She already knew who it was somehow. A sense in the air. The particular rhythm of the knock. She closed the book deliberately and rose slowly, smoothing her skirts, more out of composure than appearance.

When she opened the door, Elijah Hart stood on the threshold, his coat damp from the persistent drizzle outside, his hat in hand. His dark hair was tousled, as if he'd been running his fingers through it, a nervous habit she'd noticed during their previous encounters. Tonight, he looked less like the stern police inspector who commanded respect at the dockside and more like a man trying to figure out where he stood in territory unmarked by any map.

"I'm sorry," he said quietly. "I should've sent word."

Nell stepped aside. "It's all right. I was working anyway."

He entered without speaking further, pausing by the desk, his gaze sweeping the room. It was neat, methodical, too tidy for someone whose thoughts were in such disarray.

"I heard," he said gently, turning to face her. "About your father." His expression carried the weight of genuine sympathy

She nodded, swallowing the lump in her throat. "The letter came a few days ago."

"I'm sorry, Nell."

There was something in the way he said her name, soft, as if afraid it might break her. She hated how much it nearly did.

"Thank you," she replied. "It was sudden. Fever. Apparently quite common out there, especially during the monsoon." The clinical details were easier to recite than to acknowledge what they meant."

He hesitated, then added, "He spoke of you often, you know. When we met, years ago. Before I transferred to the river police." His eyes took on a distant look, remembering. "Said you had the sense of a harbourmaster and the temper of a gale. That if you'd been born a son, you'd have captained your own ship by twenty."

She let out a short breath, somewhere between a laugh and a sob. "That sounds like him."

Silence stretched between them, not awkward, just full. She didn't want to cry in front of him.

He stepped closer. "How are you really?"

"I'm holding things together." She gestured vaguely to the ledgers and correspondence. "The shipment from Bristol arrived yesterday. The Amsterdam consignment leaves on Tuesday."

"That's not the same as being all right." His gaze was steady, too perceptive.

She turned away from him, moving to adjust a stack of paperwork that didn't need adjusting. "There's no room for grief in a business like this. Things need signing. Men need paying."

"You've kept it all going."

"Barely."

He was quiet for a moment, then said, "I stopped by for another reason, too."

She tensed. "Go on."

"There's word," he said carefully. "You've been helping the *Eleanor* families. Quietly. Generously."

"The men served my father loyally. He would have wanted them taken care of."

"You said before you found an old account, your father's?"

"Yes." She met his gaze steadily. "A contingency fund."

"You're sure it wasn't something else?"

Her eyes snapped to his. "What are you asking me, Inspector?"

Elijah hesitated. Not because he didn't know what he wanted to say, but because he didn't want to wound her.

"I'm asking if you've made any decisions you'll

regret."

Nell's heart gave a quiet lurch. The question was too close. Too kind. It would've been easier if he'd barked it, accused her like others would have.

She drew herself up. "I'm doing what I can. That's all."

He nodded slowly. "I believe you. Or at least... I want to."

That hurt more than any accusation might have. The understanding that he was torn between his duty and his heart. Between the inspector sworn to uphold the law and the man who looked at her with undisguised tenderness.

They stood in the thick, silent space.

Then Elijah stepped back, placing his hat on his head. "If you need anything," he said, his voice low, "you only have to ask."

Nell nodded. "Thank you."

He reached for the door, paused. "I meant what I said the other day. I trust you."

She couldn't answer. Didn't deserve to. Not with the contents of Mei Ling's envelope still burning a hole in her desk drawer. Not with Jonny Collins's coded document tucked between the ledgers.

He left without pressing her further.

Nell sat down again once the door closed. The

sound of his boots on the flagstones faded into nothing.

She stared at the cold fireplace, the empty desk, the ledger full of numbers that no longer added up to the life she thought she'd been living.

And for a long time, she didn't move at all.

CHAPTER 11

Nell was bent over the ledger at her office desk, making a fresh attempt to reconcile the dock records from the *Lotus Pearl*. Outside, the distant blast of ship horns formed a background melody to her growing frustration.

The numbers still didn't add up. Three crates logged as delivered, two signed off by the customs officer, four accounted for in storage.

Four.

She frowned, tapping her pencil against the margin. Either someone had duplicated the paperwork, or something had been removed and replaced. Neither option suggested anything legitimate.

Before she could dig further, a knock sounded at

THE DOCKLAND ORPHAN

the door, too confident to be one of the dock hands seeking instruction.

She had just enough time to school her expression before the door swung open.

Elijah Hart stepped inside, his uniform coat crisp despite the damp spring weather.

"Miss Warrington," he said, nodding as he removed his hat. "Forgive the interruption."

Nell rose from her chair, spine straightening. "Inspector. Twice in one week? You must be concerned about something."

He offered a ghost of a smile, but it didn't reach his eyes. "Call it a hunch."

She forced a polite smile. "Then you'd better follow it through. Tea?" She gestured to the small pot warming on the brazier in the corner.

He declined with a slight shake of his head. "Can we go down to the warehouse?" It wasn't a question, so Nell followed him down the stairs.

He pushed the warehouse door open and glanced at the stacked boxes along the warehouse wall. His gaze lingered just a fraction too long on the ones marked with red chalk—the recent arrivals from the *Lotus Pearl*. "I was in the area," he said, each word measured and deliberate. "Thought I'd stop by."

Nell's fingers itched. She didn't believe that for a

second. Elijah Hart didn't just happen to be anywhere.

"I imagine that's rarely true," she said evenly, meeting his gaze with practiced composure. "A man in your position doesn't wander without purpose."

"No harm in checking," he replied. "With the fires. The clampdowns. We're stretched thin. Too many questions and not enough honest answers."

He moved toward a crate by the door, medium-sized, plain pine with reinforced corners, one of dozens from the *Lotus Pearl* that had arrived three days earlier. She felt her stomach tighten as his hand hovered over the lid.

"That one's already been signed off," she said lightly, striving to keep her voice casual. "Paperwork's in the logbook. Chinese silks bound for Manchester, if I'm not mistaken."

"I know," he said. "I saw the mark." He tapped the small wax seal bearing the customs officer's stamp. "Dawkins, wasn't it? New man. Efficient."

He crouched anyway, fingers brushing along the wood near the seal. There was a faint smear—residue from a removed wax seal, perhaps. Or nothing at all.

But Elijah didn't look like a man who believed in coincidences.

Nell stepped forward quickly, the rustle of her skirts too loud in the silence. "Inspector, if you're going to start inspecting private cargo, I'm afraid I'll need to see a warrant." Her voice had taken on an edge she instantly regretted, too defensive, too revealing.

He looked up at her from his crouched position. Not angry. Just... thoughtful. Measuring. As if cataloguing her reaction for future reference. "Are you always this formal with old friends?"

"I'm this formal with people who treat me like a suspect." The words were out before she could moderate them.

A pause.

He rose slowly. "You said something the other day that stuck with me."

"Oh?" She tried to recall their last conversation—which lies she'd told, which truths she'd allowed to slip through.

"You said you were managing. That there was always something." His eyes, a deep blue she'd once found comforting, now seemed to peer straight through her carefully constructed facade. "Some way to make ends meet."

She said nothing, afraid that any response would be the wrong one.

"I believed you," he said, voice lower now. "Because I wanted to. Still do. But you're acting like someone who's afraid the truth is getting too close."

Her breath caught in her throat.

"Elijah," she said softly, using his given name for the first time that day, "please, don't." The plea hung between them, loaded with meanings.

"I'm not here to accuse you," he said, his expression softening slightly. "But I need to know if you're safe. If you're still in control of this." He gestured vaguely at the warehouse, the ledgers, the whole operation she'd inherited.

"I am."

He studied her with the quiet intensity that had first drawn her to him months ago. "Then you should know, there's talk. About your dockmen. About certain crates moving through this place at night."

She stiffened.

"You need to keep your eyes open," he added. "Whatever you think you're handling… it might already be handling you."

They stood in silence for a long beat, the air thick with everything left unsaid.

Then he tipped his head. "Take care, Miss Warrington."

He left her standing in the doorway, heart pounding.

Nell waited until she was sure Elijah had gone before she turned the key in the lock. She pressed her ear to the door, holding her breath, listening for his footsteps fading into the distance. Only when she was certain did she allow herself to exhale.

The crate he'd inspected stood exactly as she'd left it, save for the faint imprint of his gloved fingers on the lid. She lifted it carefully again, muscles tensed as if expecting something, or someone, to spring from inside.

Nothing greeted her but emptiness.

She dug deeper this time, fingers sifting through the folded linen and straw packing material, pushing aside the legitimate shipment contents with growing desperation.

Still nothing.

Not even a trace of where the merchandise had been. No carefully sealed packets of fine powder. No false bottom hiding contraband. No secret compartment built into the sides. Just... gone. As if it had never existed.

Her stomach twisted into a tight knot of dread. Someone had moved it. Someone who'd known he was coming. Someone who had access to her warehouse, her shipments, her trust.

She glanced around the warehouse, heart drumming. Everything looked the same. Familiar. But suddenly, the faces in her mind blurred at the edges, men she thought she trusted. Men who smiled and nodded and took their pay each week without question.

But one of them had known.

She crossed to the ledger desk, flipping through the most recent delivery logs, fingers scanning quickly for discrepancies.

She grabbed the dock register and began pulling sheets, checking signatures. A few were off, careless squiggles where there had once been neat initials. One had clearly been forged. She recognised the hand. It belonged to Jack Blythe, one of the younger dockhands, always loud, always late, always bragging about things he shouldn't have had money for.

And then there was Thomas, older, steady, someone she'd trusted with small errands for years. But lately, he'd been quiet. Watchful. And he'd started showing up to work in boots that looked far too new for a man with seven children.

Nell pressed a hand to her forehead. The floor seemed to shift beneath her feet.

She didn't know who was working for her anymore. Or worse, who was working against her. Who had allied themselves with rival interests. Who might be informing on her to the authorities, to Elijah's superiors, if not Elijah himself.

And Elijah had seen it. The crate. Her fear. Her lies, even if he hadn't named them yet. He was no fool. It was one of the things that had drawn her to him before everything had changed.

She slammed the ledger shut and paced the office, trying to contain the rising panic.

Jonny had told her she was protected. Mei had told her she was reckless. And now she didn't know who to believe, herself least of all.

There was a knock on the warehouse side door. Just one. Sharp and deliberate.

She didn't answer it. She couldn't.

Not until she figured out which side she was on. Not until she could look Elijah Hart in the eye without flinching.

Her mind raced through possibilities, each one more precarious than the last, searching desperately for her next course of action. The warehouse no longer felt safe, not with unknown eyes watching, unknown hands moving her shipments, unknown loyalties shifting. There was only one person she could speak honestly with now, one person who understood the true nature of the web she'd entangled herself in.

She grabbed her shawl, slipped out the rear entrance of the warehouse and started towards the Chinese Quarter.

Mei Ling didn't look surprised when Nell walked into the apothecary without knocking. The small shop was empty of customers, the air heavy with the scent of dried herbs and roots that hung from the ceiling in neat bunches.

The bell above the door gave its customary chime, but Mei didn't glance up from her mortar and pestle. She continued grinding a mixture of dried roots, her movements smooth and unhurried.

"I thought you might come," she said softly.

Nell shut the door behind her, turning the sign from "Open" to "Closed" with a decisive flip. "Then you know."

Mei gave a small nod, still focused on her work. "Something's gone wrong." It wasn't a question.

"Someone moved one of the crates," Nell said, her voice low. "Before Elijah arrived. The contents are gone."

Mei poured the crushed herbs into a pouch. "And he noticed?"

"He noticed everything." Nell crossed the shop in two strides. "You didn't warn anyone? Tell the porters to keep it tight?"

"I told no one," Mei said calmly, tying the pouch with a red string. "Because there was no one to tell. The porters were instructed to handle the crates as usual. Business as ordinary. Draw no attention."

Nell leaned on the counter, voice sharpening. "Then someone else did. Someone inside the warehouse. Maybe more than one."

Mei's expression didn't change, but something in her eyes hardened. "Then your circle is no longer closed."

"I thought it was," Nell said, too fast, too desperate. "I trusted them. I've known these men for years. Some worked for my father."

Mei arched one delicate brow. "Trust is a luxury, Nell. Not a currency."

"That's not helpful."

"I'm not trying to be."

A silence stretched between them, filled only by the ticking of the wall clock and the soft hum of life outside the shop.

Mei sighed and set the pouch aside, folding her hands on the counter. "You've brought in people you can't control."

Nell knew where this was going. The warning Mei had given her weeks ago when she'd first mentioned Jonny's proposal. "You mean Jonny."

"I mean whoever Jonny brings with him," Mei said. "You think he's the extent of the risk, but he's just the charming face at the front of a much darker machine."

"He's helped me," Nell said defensively. "He's kept things moving. Kept us—"

"Lucky," Mei cut in. "For now."

Nell looked away.

"You're not stupid," Mei continued, softer now. "But you're tired. And you're grieving. And he knows it."

Nell pressed her fingers to her temple. "You think I've lost control."

"I think," Mei said carefully, "that you never had it. Not fully. Not once Jonny made this about more than one shipment. Men like him offer a hand to help you across the stream, but they're really just pulling you into deeper water."

"And what would you have me do?" Nell snapped. "Go to the Inspector? Tell him everything? Let him hand me over for a neat confession?"

Mei's gaze darkened. "If you wait too long,

someone else will hand you over first. "Someone who needs to save themselves."

Nell stared at her, throat tight.

"I can't protect you from men I don't know," Mei said. "And I won't risk the shop. My people. My family."

"I'm not asking you to," Nell said quietly. "I just… needed someone to tell me I'm not losing my mind."

"You're not," Mei said. "But you're standing on the edge of it."

Nell took a shaky breath. "What would you do?"

Mei looked at her for a long moment, then said, "I'd choose who I trust. Now. Before someone else chooses for me. And I'd remember that men like Collins are not loyal to people. They're loyal to profit. To power."

Her eyes held Nell's with unwavering intensity. "Inspector Hart, for all his rigid principles… at least his honour isn't for sale to the highest bidder."

Nell swallowed hard, unable to dispute the truth in Mei's words. "And if I choose wrong?"

"Then we will not speak again," Mei said simply, stepping back. "For both our sakes."

When Nell returned, the warehouse was quiet. Too quiet.

She stood by the open ledger on her desk, the

pages fluttering faintly in the breeze from the open window.

She stared at the scrawled signatures on the page, names she'd trusted. The records had been altered. Just enough to slip through if no one was paying attention.

But Elijah had paid attention. And now she couldn't stop thinking about the way he'd looked at her. Not with suspicion exactly, but with something worse.

Disappointment.

She pushed the ledger away and moved to the window, arms wrapped tightly around herself.

Out on the docks, shadows moved. Men hauling crates, calling to one another in low voices. Honest work. Dishonest cargo.

Her father had once told her, *"There's no shame in hard work. But there's shame in cheating a man who trusts you."*

And Elijah trusted her.

Or had.

She pressed her forehead to the pane.

Everything had felt so simple at first. One shipment. Then another. Then a dozen. The lies had layered themselves like silt on the riverbed, and now she could no longer see the bottom.

Mei was right. Jonny had changed the game. She'd let him. His charm, his swagger, his promises of protection and control. But now she didn't know who he worked for... or what they might demand of her next.

And Mei, once her calm in the storm, was growing distant. Frustrated. The rules were changing too fast, and Nell no longer knew where the lines were drawn.

She turned from the window, pacing the floor.

She could try to wrestle it back under control. Push Jonny out. Re-establish boundaries. But who would follow her now? Who, among the men who smiled and nodded and quietly betrayed her, would still listen?

The only person she could even think of was Elijah.

And he was slipping away too.

But maybe it wasn't too late. If she told him the truth. Not all of it. But enough. Enough to let him help her before it was too far gone.

Her gut twisted.

He'd hate her for the lies. But if he knew what she was trying to fix, what she was trying to stop, would he still come? Would he still choose her?

She didn't know.

She only knew that the business her father left behind had become something he wouldn't recognise.

And if she didn't do something soon, it would destroy it, and her, in the process.

She sat at the desk, staring at the open drawer where her father's last letter still lay.

"You're stronger than you think."

Her hand trembled as she reached for it.

For the first time, she wasn't sure he'd been right.

CHAPTER 12

The morning mist clung low over the Thames, curling between the crates and cobblestones. Nell stepped out of the cab and wrapped her cloak tighter around her shoulders. The streets were still sleepy, the usual dockside bustle not yet in full swing.

But something was wrong.

Voices drifted through the fog, low and urgent. As she turned the corner toward her office, she saw the crowd.

A small group of dockworkers huddled near the edge of the wharf, their caps in their hands, blocking the view of the river. Two men knelt beside something on the ground, their faces grim in the grey morning light.

Her pace quickened.

"Oi, back up, give him space," someone barked. "He's gone, you idiot, he don't need space—"

"What's happened?" Nell asked as she pushed her way forward.

The men stepped aside just enough to let her through.

That's when she saw him.

Jack Blythe.

His body lay crumpled near a stack of mooring ropes, one arm crooked beneath him at an unnatural angle. His lips were tinged blue, his eyes glassy and open, staring up at nothing. A thin trail of dried foam marked the corner of his mouth.

Someone had draped a rough blanket over his lower half, but it did nothing to soften the reality of what had happened.

A younger dockhand, Charlie, she thought, stood nearby, pale and shaken.

"Found him just now, Miss," he said. "Floating in the shallows. Looks like he went in sometime last night. Slipped, maybe. Or—"

Nell crouched beside the body, her eyes drawn to the object clutched in Jack's right hand.

A small glass vial. Stoppered, but empty. The inside was faintly stained with a brownish residue.

She didn't need to smell it to know what it had been.

Opium. Strong. Possibly cut with something else. Something cheaper. Something deadly.

Her throat tightened.

"How did he even get it?" she asked, mostly to herself.

One of the older men shifted uncomfortably. "Jack's been odd lately. Flashing cash, whisperin' to blokes from outside the yards. Thought he'd got himself a side hustle. Didn't think it was... this."

Nell stood slowly. "Did he say where it came from?"

Mick shook his head. "Didn't have time to ask. Now he won't be answering anything."

She stepped back, her hands shaking, not just from the cold.

The crowd was watching her. Not with accusation exactly, but something close. Apprehension. Expectation. As if they knew her hands weren't clean, but didn't know what to say.

She turned without another word and walked toward her office.

Once inside, she closed the door and pressed her back against it, her breath shaky. Her eyes stung but didn't spill.

This was never supposed to happen.

It had been business. Just business. Keeping the company afloat. Helping the widows. Protecting what her father had built.

But Jack was dead.

And that vial had looked very much like the ones Mei's men packed in secret compartments beneath innocent cargo.

Except Mei would never make it sloppy.

Which meant… someone else had supplied him.

Or worse, someone had tampered with their shipment.

And now a man was dead. On her watch. With her name stamped on every crate in the yard.

She snatched up her skirts and strode out the back door, flagging down a passing cab to take her to the Chinese Quarter.

The trip passed in a blur of crowded streets and grey buildings, her mind racing faster than the horse that pulled them.

The apothecary was still shuttered when Nell arrived.

She knocked once. Then again, with urgency. Her heartbeat pounded in her ears, and her coat was damp from the river mist.

A minute passed before the bolts slid back. Mei

opened the door in her dressing gown, hair pinned loosely, a single oil lamp flickering behind her.

"Is someone dead?" she asked dryly, clearly annoyed at the early disturbance.

"Yes," Nell said, the word landing between them like a dropped stone.

That wiped the sarcasm from her face.

She stepped back silently to let Nell in, locking the door behind them.

"Who?"

"Jack Blythe."

Mei blinked. "One of your men?"

Nell nodded, unwinding her scarf with trembling fingers. "He overdosed. Found floating by the moorings this morning. Blue-lipped and stiff."

Mei didn't speak for a moment. Then, calmly: "Do you want tea?"

"No, Mei, I don't want bloody tea—" Nell cut herself off, running a hand through her damp hair. "He had a vial on him. Looked just like ours. Same size. Same seal. Same residue."

Mei's jaw tightened. "Then it wasn't from me."

"You can't be sure."

"I can." Mei turned away, disappearing into the back room. Nell followed, heels echoing too loudly on the wooden floor.

"He had product, Mei," she said. "And he's dead. That makes us murderers."

"No," Mei replied. "That makes someone a murderer. But not us."

Nell's voice cracked. "How can you say that? You didn't see his face—"

"I've seen too many like it," Mei said, her voice still maddeningly calm. "And I've made it my business never to supply cut opium. My batches are clean. That's the only reason I agreed to this at all."

"Then who gave it to him?"

Mei looked at her. "You really need me to say it?"

Nell felt the answer before it came.

"Jonny."

Mei nodded. "Or one of his men. Maybe not directly, but someone he let too close. Someone who doesn't care about caution or quality. Someone who sees this as just another trade."

She narrowed her eyes, knowing her words would break Nell's heart but speaking them anyway. The truth between them had always been their currency.

"It's an easy make Nell. Jonny knows which crates have the product, it's very easy to swap them with cut opium and sell the better product on the market for more. My guess is Jack was on the make too, taking the odd vial here and there. This time he took the wrong one."

Nell's hands curled into fists. "Jonny told me I was protected."

Mei raised an eyebrow. "You are. From the police. From customs. From fire. But not from rot."

They stared at one another across the shadowy counter.

"I need to get out of this," Nell said. "Before it destroys everything."

Mei leaned forward slightly. "Then stop pretending you still have control. That ended weeks ago."

Nell swallowed hard. "He knows something's wrong. Elijah."

Mei's expression softened, just a little. "Then tell him."

"I can't. He's a good man. The only one left, it seems." The unspoken hung between them, that Elijah might not love her if he knew what she'd become.

"Then don't be surprised when he finds out anyway."

The words landed like stones in her chest.

"Just... be careful, Nell," Mei added. "The moment people start dying, the rules change. People don't just cover tracks, they start burning bridges. You're standing on one now."

Nell looked down, breathing through her teeth.

"I didn't ask for this," she murmured.

"No," Mei said. "But you said yes."

"I need to talk to Jonny," she said, her voice steadier than she felt. "Tonight."

The tavern on Gunner's Row was half-empty by the time Nell pushed open the door. The usual smell of pipe smoke hung in the air, mingling with the stale scent of beer and old sweat.

A handful of dockmen played cards in the back corner, their rough voices occasionally punctuated by curses or barks of laughter. The barkeep eyed her with mild curiosity. Women of her station rarely entered such establishments, especially alone, but no one else looked up when she entered.

Jonny Collins was already waiting, slouched in a booth near the hearth, boots up on the opposite bench, coat unbuttoned like he owned the place.

She didn't wait to be invited. She slid into the seat across from him and slammed her leather gloves down on the table with enough force to make the nearby candle flicker.

His grin widened. "Evening, sunshine. What brings a lady to this fine establishment?"

"Don't," she snapped. "Not today."

Jonny tilted his head, the grin lingering. "Problem?"

"You know why I'm here." Her hands remained flat on the table, refusing to fidget despite the urge.

"I might. But please," he gestured grandly, "enlighten me."

"Jack Blythe is dead," she said. "Overdose. They found a vial on him. It looked a lot like ours."

His expression flickered, just a beat, but he recovered quickly, lounging back. "Tragic. But hardly my fault."

"You sure about that?" She leaned forward, lowering her voice. "Because it seems like an awfully strange coincidence."

He held her gaze, suddenly very still, all traces of the charming rogue vanishing. Something colder took its place. "You accusing me of something, sweetheart?"

"Don't call me that."

"Fine." He leaned forward, resting his elbows on the table. "You think I handed Jack a poisoned vial and told him to snort his way into the afterlife?"

"I think you've been switching product. That your people are sloppy. And that someone in your chain doesn't give a damn about quality."

Jonny let out a slow, sharp breath. "You want to do this here, in public?"

"There's no one listening."

He glanced around. A barkeep wiping down mugs. A drunk asleep near the door. The card players murmuring over their hands.

"Look," he said, lowering his voice, "Jack was a good kid. Loud, stupid, but decent. But he was also greedy. Always sniffing after side deals. If he got his hands on something bad, it wasn't through me."

"And I'm just supposed to take your word for it?"

"You've taken it before." His eyes flicked down to her lips, then back up. "In matters far more personal."

She flinched, the memory of his hands on her skin rising despite herself.

He softened his tone. "Come on, Nell. You know me. You know I wouldn't risk the entire operation on one idiot worker with a death wish."

"I also know you've been getting bold," she said. "More hands in the pot. You've expanded, and you didn't tell me."

His smile turned cold, all pretence of charm vanishing. "That's rich. Coming from the girl who begged for help when she was drowning in her daddy's debts. When the company was weeks from collapse."

Nell stood abruptly, the legs of her chair scraping against the rough wooden floor. "I didn't beg."

"No," he said, rising to face her. "You flirted. You let me in. You let me save your skin. And now that it's uncomfortable, you want to pretend you're still calling the shots."

Her heart thundered, but she didn't step back.

"This stops now," she said, each word precise and cold. "No more expansion. No more crates. I want out."

Jonny studied her for a moment, his eyes tracing the contours of her face as if memorizing them, then gave a low, humorless chuckle that raised the hairs on the back of her neck.

"Oh, darling," he said, the endearment dripping with condescension. "You're not out. You're in. You're the pretty front of the whole thing. The respectable name. The one the customs officers trust. The one the Inspector doesn't want to suspect. You're the perfect camouflage." He reached out to touch her cheek. "And that makes you more valuable than you know."

She slapped him. Hard. The sound cracked through the tavern like a gunshot.

His jaw tightened, but he didn't raise a hand in return. He just smiled again, slower this time. Meaner.

"There she is," he murmured. "I knew she'd show up eventually."

She turned on her heel and walked out, her hands shaking, bile rising in her throat.

Outside, the night was wet and cold. A fine mist had begun to fall, smothering all around it.

Behind her, Jonny's voice floated out the door. "Careful, Nell. You start torching bridges, you'd better make damn sure you don't still need to cross them."

She didn't look back. She hailed a cab, desperate for the comfort of home and somewhere safe to get her thoughts straight.

As she climbed in, she caught sight of Jonny framed in the tavern doorway, watching her go, his expression unreadable in the mist.

"Islington," she told the driver. "Pembroke Street."

The house in Islington was quiet when she arrived, save for the soft crackle of the fire that Mrs. Hudson had thoughtfully lit before retiring for the evening, and the occasional solemn tick from the grandfather clock in the hallway. Nell hadn't bothered to light the lamps. She sat curled in the armchair by the grate, legs tucked beneath her, the hem of her dress still damp from the mist, her hair falling loose from its pins.

She hadn't eaten. Couldn't. The thought of food made her stomach turn.

Jonny's words still echoed in her ears. So did Jack's name. And the look on Mei's face when she'd said, *"You didn't stop it either."*

She was tired in a way that sleep couldn't fix.

So when the knock came, she flinched.

Three measured raps. Not urgent. Not timid.

Elijah.

She hesitated only a moment before crossing the room and opening the door, not bothering to check her appearance in the hallway mirror. What did it matter now?

He stood with his hat in his hands, coat buttoned against the drizzle, and a look in his eyes that wasn't quite businesslike.

"I hope I'm not intruding," he said softly.

She opened the door wider. "You're not."

He stepped inside, and she led him to the drawing room, neither speaking until the firelight flickered between them.

"I heard," he said after a pause. "About Jack."

Nell nodded, throat too tight to answer. Of

course he had heard. Little happened on the docks that Inspector Elijah Ward didn't eventually learn of.

"I thought you might want someone to talk to."

She gave a bitter little smile. "Is that an official offer? From the Metropolitan Police?"

He shook his head. "From someone who's worried about you."

She swallowed hard, then looked away, unable to bear the genuine concern in his gaze. She didn't deserve it. "He was just a boy. Loud, annoying. Always chewing something. But he didn't deserve that."

"No. He didn't."

"He had a sister," Nell whispered. "I met her once. She was deaf. He said he was saving up to send her to a proper school."

Elijah's expression flickered with quiet pain.

"I should've…" She stopped herself. "I keep thinking I could've done something."

He leaned forward slightly. "I don't know what you're caught up in, Nell. I won't pretend I don't see the signs. The sudden financial recovery of your company. The new associates. The late-night meetings." His eyes held hers, unflinching but without accusation. "But I also see someone trying to do good, even when the world keeps backing her into corners.

She blinked fast, hating the burn behind her eyes.

"You don't know everything," she said, her voice barely above a whisper.

"Then tell me," he said, gently. An invitation, not a demand. The inspector set aside for the man.

She looked at him, really looked, at the steadiness in his eyes, the softness that made her want to believe he meant it. That maybe he wouldn't judge her too harshly. That maybe she wasn't entirely lost, beyond redemption.

"I can't," she said. "Not yet."

He nodded once. "Then I'll wait."

A silence settled between them, not uncomfortable this time, just... close.

Elijah stood, smoothing the brim of his hat with long, elegant fingers. "I should go. It's late. But I'll be nearby, if you need me."

She rose with him, brushing a lock of hair from her face, suddenly aware of her disheveled appearance. "Thank you. For checking on me."

"Elijah—" she said, and didn't know what came after that.

He turned and took her hand in his, colour creeping up his neck at the boldness of his move.

She didn't pull away, glad to feel the warmth of human contact that asked nothing of her, demanded nothing. A feeling of safety washed over her, brief but profound.

"I'll be nearby," he repeated, quieter this time. His thumb brushed over her knuckles once, a gesture so tender she felt tears spring in her eyes.

And then he was gone, his boots echoing down the steps, swallowed by the mist.

Nell stood by the door long after he'd disappeared from view.

It was the first time in weeks she'd felt like someone still saw the version of her she used to be.

And it made her want to be that woman again—before it was too late.

CHAPTER 13

The mist clung to the edges of the warehouse, shrouding it in secrecy. Nell stood just outside the office door, her gloved fingers smudged with ink from the manifest she'd been reviewing. The leather-bound ledger felt heavier with each passing day, weighted by numbers that didn't quite add up and shipments that arrived with contents she deliberately avoided inspecting too closely.

The morning deliveries had come in late, and half her mind was preoccupied with rearranging schedules and docking slips.

That's when she noticed him.

A man, mid-forties, in a grey suit that didn't quite

match the grime of the docks, was leaning against a crate a few yards off, watching her.

He smiled when their eyes met. Not kindly.

"Miss Warrington," he said, straightening and strolling toward her with the casual confidence of someone who believed himself indispensable. "A word, if I may."

Nell stiffened, her shoulders pulling back in a defensive posture. "I'm rather busy, as you can see. Perhaps you could schedule an appointment."

He pulled a card from his pocket, glancing at it more than handing it over. "Mr Greeley. Harbour Licensing Office. I just happened to be passing by. Thought I'd offer my congratulations."

"Congratulations?" Nell didn't reach for the card. She knew what it would say. A title that sounded official enough to intimidate those who didn't know better, but vague enough to mean nothing at all.

"Well, your little operation's grown so much in the last few months. His gaze swept across the yard, taking in the stacks of crates, the workers hauling cargo, the ships moored at her piers. "So many new faces. Such interesting shipments. From China, I understand. And the Americas." He turned back to her, eyes cold despite his smile. "It's always good to see a young woman succeeding in a man's world.

Impressive, really, how quickly you've managed to... expand."

The way he said it made her skin crawl.

"If you have a question about licensing," Nell said, keeping her tone crisp, "you can speak to my representative."

He tutted lightly, the sound condescending. "No need for all that, Miss Warrington. Legal proceedings are so tedious, don't you find? I'm not here to make trouble. But let's say... some of your more adventurous arrangements have come to the attention of certain departments. Departments that like to be reassured that everything is being conducted... properly."

"What are you implying?" She kept her voice steady despite the dread pooling in her stomach.

"Nothing at all." He held up his hands in a gesture of mock innocence. "Consider me a friend. One who can ensure that certain irregularities in your manifests, a missing crate here, an undeclared shipment there, don't find their way into official reports. But perhaps a gesture... a small monthly sum... would ensure no unnecessary scrutiny. We all want to avoid unpleasant paperwork, don't we?"

Nell's stomach turned. This wasn't a request. It was a threat, plain and simple.

She glanced around, noting with dismay that several workers had drifted away from their tasks, sensing the tension even if they couldn't hear the words.

For a moment, she considered refusing. Calling his bluff. But if he did work for the Harbour Authority, or worse, if he had connections higher up, he could bring everything crashing down with a single report.

She reached for her purse with shaking hands she couldn't quite steady, pulling a few folded notes from the inner pocket and pressing them into his waiting palm.

"That's all I have on me," she said, voice low. "Take it. But you come here again, and I'll report you myself."

Mr Greeley tucked the notes away with a sly smile. "Consider this a courtesy call. A little taste of what's to come. Next time, it won't be so polite. Or so cheap."

His gaze traveled over her form in a way that suggested he wasn't just interested in her money. "Though I'd be open to... alternative arrangements, if you find yourself short on funds."

She recoiled, disgust flooding her veins. "Get off my property."

"For now." He tipped his hat with mocking deference. "I'll be in touch."

He turned and strolled away into the fog as though they'd simply been exchanging pleasantries.

Nell stood motionless, heart pounding, the docks spinning slightly around her as she tried to catch her breath. This wasn't just whispers now. This wasn't just Jonny and his rough men, or Mei and her quiet warnings. This was blackmail. Exposure.

And she didn't know who to turn to.

The next morning, the office felt colder than usual, the fog pressing against the windows as if the docks themselves were closing in. Nell sat hunched at her desk, elbows planted firmly beside the ledger she wasn't reading. She'd been sitting there for an hour, but had written nothing. The numbers swam. Her focus was shot. All she could think about was Greeley's smirk, his oily voice, the way he'd folded her money with slow, deliberate fingers.

The door creaked open. She didn't look up.

"I heard you had a visitor," Jonny said.

His voice always brought a reaction. She hated that.

Nell exhaled and raised her eyes. He was already inside, shrugging off his coat like he owned the place, his smile easy and unreadable.

"Word spreads fast," she said dryly, leaning back in her chair.

"In my line of work? It has to."

He dropped into the chair opposite her and stretched his legs. He didn't ask permission.

"Who told you?" she asked, fingers drumming once against the closed ledger.

"I've got ears all over these docks. You know that." He watched her too carefully, like he was cataloguing every twitch of her expression. "The harbormaster's boy saw him leaving. Said Greeley looked mighty pleased with himself."

She snapped the ledger shut with more force than necessary. "Then you also know he tried to extort me."

Jonny's smile faded, something cold and calculating replacing it. "He put his hands on you?"

"No." Her voice faltered. "Not like that. But he made it clear he'd seen too much. And that he wouldn't keep quiet unless I paid."

Jonny leaned back, studying her. The easy charm vanished, replaced by something harder. "And you did?"

She nodded once, jaw tight. "Just enough to get him to leave."

Jonny let out a low whistle and shook his head. "That was your first mistake."

"I didn't ask for your opinion, Jonny." The words came out sharper than she intended.

He stood up abruptly, the chair scraping against the floorboards. "I'm giving it anyway."

She stood too, unwilling to let him tower over her, voice rising. "I handled it."

"No, sweetheart," he said coolly, stepping closer, "you postponed it. You fed the rat. Now he'll be back with more teeth."

Jonny tilted his head, the ghost of a smile touching his lips. "You wanted protection. I promised it. This is what that looks like."

She stared at him, her hands tightening at her sides, nails biting into her palms. "What are you going to do?"

"Nothing that'll come back on you," he said, softer now. "I'll make sure he forgets your name. That's all."

She didn't trust him, not entirely. But something about the way he said it, quiet and sure, made her chest twist.

"Jonny…"

He reached out suddenly and tucked a loose curl behind her ear. His touch was light. Possessive.

"You don't have to worry about worms like him," he said. "Not while I'm breathing."

He left before she could argue further, the door clicking shut behind him with quiet finality.

The next morning, Nell heard the whispers long before anyone told her outright.

The docks were a rumour mill, especially when violence was involved. She passed two labourers murmuring near the hoist, their voices dropping as she approached. Another man gave her a stiff nod and quickly walked the other way.

By midafternoon, the knot in her stomach had tightened to the point of nausea. Something had happened. Something she had set in motion.

When George finally knocked on the warehouse office door, his cap twisted nervously in his weathered hands, she knew what he was going to say before he opened his mouth.

"They found him, miss. Greeley. Down by the alley behind the Sailor's Rest."

She set her pen down slowly, the metal nib scratching against the paper. "Found him?"

George shifted his weight, eyes fixed somewhere over her left shoulder. "Beaten, miss. Face bloodied something awful. Arm snapped clean through, they say." He swallowed visibly. "Three broken ribs.

Blind in one eye now, maybe permanent. Nothing taken, though. Watch and wallet still there. Not a robbery."

Nell's stomach dropped, a cold wave washing through her. She gripped the edge of the desk to steady herself.

"Thank you, George. That'll be all."

He left without another word.

She stared at the wall for a long time, seeing nothing.

She knew. She didn't want to believe it, but she knew. This was the cost of the bargain she'd made months ago, when the ledgers wouldn't balance and the creditors were circling. When Jonny had appeared with his easy smile and easier solutions.

When the door opened again half an hour later, she didn't need to look up to know it was him. The scent of rain and tobacco announced his presence before his footsteps did.

Jonny stepped inside, calm and casual as always, brushing the rain from his coat sleeves. His knuckles weren't even bruised. Of course not. He wouldn't do the work himself.

"You're welcome," he said, voice light, as if he'd done her a simple favour.

Nell turned to face him slowly. Her throat felt

like it had closed over, words struggling to form. "You... did that?"

He arched a brow, looking almost amused. "I told you I'd take care of it."

She rose from her desk, voice shaking. "You didn't say you'd send someone to— to break his bones!"

He shrugged, so nonchalant it made her blood boil. "Didn't think you needed the details."

"God, Jonny, he's a civil servant. This isn't some backroom turf squabble between your kind. You've drawn blood now."

He stepped closer, voice cool. "He tried to blackmail you. That makes him a threat. And I said—" He leaned in, expression suddenly sharp. "No one threatens you while I'm around."

She took a step back, heart thudding.

"There were other ways—"

"Were there?" he snapped, the first real crack in his composure. "You think handing him a few crumpled notes was going to make him forget what he saw? You think a man like that stops at one payment?" He shook his head, a humorless laugh escaping him. "You're in this now, Nell. All the way in. You can't throw money at problems and expect them to stay away."

She shook her head, struggling to breathe.

"This wasn't protection," she whispered. "It was a message."

He smiled faintly, something like approval flickering in his eyes. "Exactly. And now he's received it. Loud and clear. So has everyone else with ideas about taking advantage of you."

She pressed a hand to her forehead, as if trying to steady herself, feeling the beginnings of a pounding headache. "I didn't ask for this."

"You did," he said gently. "The minute you took that first shipment. The minute you let me in. You wanted protection. This is what it looks like."

Her eyes met his, angry, hurt, uncertain. And for a moment, he looked almost regretful. But then it was gone, replaced by that familiar, impenetrable mask.

"Still," he added, "I didn't want you to worry."

He turned and left, the soft click of the door closing behind him, leaving her alone with her thoughts.

The business she'd fought to keep afloat after her father's death was changing into something unrecognisable, something darker.

Was this what safety looked like now?

Was this what she had become?

The knock came just after dusk, three precise taps that seemed to reverberate through the quiet house.

Nell didn't answer it right away. She stood frozen in the hallway of the Islington house, staring at the door as though she might will the visitor away. The letter from her father still lay open on the writing desk in the next room, its yellowed edges curling slightly in the damp evening air. Words of pride and trust, written in his steady hand, now tainted by everything she'd done since it arrived six months ago.

I know you'll take care of the business with the same integrity I've always tried to show...

She straightened her spine and opened the door slowly.

Elijah stood there in his overcoat, rain beading on the dark wool. His expression was unreadable, but his eyes were troubled. His hair was damp from the drizzle, a darker shade of brown than usual. He didn't offer a smile, and that told her everything she needed to know about why he'd come.

"May I come in?" His voice was formal, the voice he used when he was trying to maintain distance.

She stepped aside without a word, her heart hammering against her ribs.

They walked to the drawing room in silence, their footsteps echoing on the wooden floor. The fire had gone low in the grate, casting shadows along the walls. Nell lit the lamp with a trembling hand, the warm glow illuminating the worry lines around Elijah's mouth as she turned to face him.

"You're here about Greeley," she said. Not a question.

He nodded, removing his hat but not sitting, as though this wasn't a visit he intended to prolong. "I take it you've heard."

"Of course I've heard. Everyone has." She kept her voice steady by sheer force of will.

She watched him carefully. He was studying her the way he always did, like she was a puzzle he was trying to solve. There was no judgment in his gaze, not yet, but there was something worse: disappointment.

"I thought you should know," he said, turning his hat in his hands, "there are whispers linking it to your warehouse. Or at least to your... company."

Nell felt the blood drain from her face, leaving her light-headed. She reached for the back of a nearby chair to steady herself. "There's no proof of that," she said, although she sounded more defeated than she intended. The words rang hollow even to her own ears.

"No," he agreed, his eyes never leaving her face. "But you and I both know that's not the same as being innocent."

The silence stretched between them. Her breath came shallow. She looked away, unable to bear the weight of his gaze any longer.

"Have you come here to accuse me?" she finally asked, raising her chin in defiance.

"No." His voice was quiet now, gentler. "I've come because I'm worried about you."

Her defenses wavered, just for a second. "You shouldn't be."

"I'm not here in uniform, Nell." He placed his hat carefully on the side table.

She finally met his eyes again.

"I know you're caught in something," he said, taking a half-step closer. "I see it every time I look at you. The shadows under your eyes. The way your smile never quite reaches your eyes anymore." He paused, his voice dropping lower. "You're drowning, and pretending not to be."

Her composure cracked like. She turned away, gripping the back of the nearest chair until her knuckles turned white, focusing on the pain to keep herself from falling apart completely.

"I don't know what to do," she whispered, the confession rising from her throat. "I'm backed into a corner. I owe people—people who don't take no for an answer. I feel like all my choices have been taken away from me, one by one, until there's nothing left but bad decisions."

"Tell me," he said, his voice an anchor. "Tell me what's going on. Who's behind this? Is it Jonny?"

Her voice broke. "I can't."

He took another step forward, close enough that she could smell the rain on his coat. "Nell—"

"I said I can't!" she cried, spinning around, her eyes bright with unshed tears. "It's too late. Everything's gone too far. I keep trying to fix it, but every choice makes it worse. One compromise leads to another, and another, until—" She broke off, hands twisting together. "I'm not who you think I am anymore, Elijah. I'm not sure I ever was."

She was sobbing now, silent, angry tears that spilled faster than she could stop them. She hated herself for this weakness, for letting him see her crumble.

Elijah didn't speak. He just stepped forward and gathered her into his arms, one hand cradling the back of her head, the other strong across her shoulders.

For a moment, Nell let herself collapse into him, his warmth, his steadiness, the safety she'd been craving. She gripped the lapel of his coat and buried her face against his shoulder, inhaling the scent of wool and rain and him.

"I didn't mean for any of this," she whispered against the fabric.

"I know," he murmured, his breath warm against her hair. "I know."

She pulled back just enough to look at him, and in the dim firelight, their faces were only inches apart. He seemed different somehow, less the stern officer and more the man she'd glimpsed in rare unguarded moments. His hand brushed her cheek, wiping away a tear with his thumb, the gesture tentative but sure. Her breath came faster, as though she couldn't get enough air, the room suddenly too warm.

Then he kissed her.

It was gentle at first, but charged with everything unsaid between them, months of conversations that skirted the edges of what they really wanted to say. Nell didn't resist. She leaned into it, her hand sliding up to the nape of his neck, fingers threading through his damp hair, needing something to feel real amid the web of lies she'd spun around herself.

When they parted, her eyes still wet with tears, she searched his face, eager to know his thoughts, his feelings, whether this changed anything between them.

Elijah looked stricken, the realisation of what he'd done dawning in his eyes. He stepped back, his hands falling away from her, suddenly remembering who he was.

"I'm sorry," he said, his voice low. "That was... I shouldn't have. Not now. Not like this."

She didn't answer, disappointment flickering in her eyes like the dying fire behind her.

He picked up his hat from the side table, the moment unraveling in his hands. "I should go."

"Elijah—" she started, but what could she say? That she wasn't involved? That she could explain? The lies stuck in her throat.

The front door closed behind him with a soft click that seemed to echo through the empty house.

Nell sank to the floor by the fireplace. She didn't try to stop the tears that fell freely now, splashing onto her dress.

She had two men offering her protection. Jonny with his dangerous charm and uncompromising methods. Elijah with his steady moral compass and genuine concern. One who would break the law to keep her safe; one who upheld it, even at personal cost.

And she knew now, with devastating clarity, that Elijah was the one she wanted.

But as the fire died, casting the room into deeper shadow, a colder realisation settled over her: This fragile feeling between them, was this yet another choice that would end in trouble for them both?

Or worse, would her connection to Jonny destroy any chance she and Elijah might have had before it even began?

She stared into the dying flames, seeing no answers in their flickering light.

CHAPTER 14

The early morning haze drifted over Limehouse like a shroud, grey and heavy with the scent of coal smoke. Gulls cried overhead, their voices mournful against the distant clang of loading cranes.

Inside the warehouse, Nell was reviewing the shipment manifest for the next delivery, trying to silence the buzz of anxiety in her chest. The previous night's conversation with Elijah echoed in her mind. His kiss, the warmth of his hands on her face, the weight of his disappointment. Worse than all that was the terrible knowledge that with every passing day, she was slipping further from the person he thought she was, the person she wanted to be.

A sharp knock broke her concentration, making her flinch.

She looked up to see Owen, one of her steadiest dockhands, hovering in the doorway. He removed his cap, twisting it in his hands.

"You need to hear something, Miss Warrington. It's about the next shipment."

Her stomach dropped. Even before he spoke, she knew. Another problem, another threat. They kept multiplying like rats in the hold. "Go on."

"There's talk on the docks," he said, glancing behind him before stepping inside. "Word is, someone's planning to intercept it. A rival crew. Not just a smash-and-grab either, proper sabotage. They're saying it's personal."

"Who's saying this?" she demanded.

Owen shifted uneasily. "Everyone and no one. Rumours, mostly. But the same name keeps coming up, Thomas Thorne. One of those East End blokes with big connections and a bigger temper. Word is, he controls half the routes north of the river now. He's been sniffing around your operation. Doesn't like that you're moving things and making money in what he considers his territory."

Nell steadied herself against a crate, the edges of

her vision tightening. She pressed her fingers to her temples.

"I thought the last shipment went through clean."

"It did. But someone's been watching. Maybe Greeley talked before... well, before what happened to him. Or maybe your name's just gotten too loud."

He hesitated, then added, "Some of the lads are jumpy. Peters quit this morning. Johnson says his wife won't let him come back after what happened to Greeley. They're saying it's not worth the coin anymore. That there's too much heat."

Nell clenched her jaw. "I understand. Tell them I'll sort it. They'll be safe."

But as Owen nodded and left, she didn't believe her own words.

For the first time, she couldn't see a way forward.

And worse, she wasn't sure who she could still trust. She grabbed her cloak, and headed for the Chinese quarter. She knew Mei Ling's patience was wearing thin with her bringing problems to her door, but there was nowhere else to turn now that Elijah wasn't an option. Not after last night. Not after that kiss that changed everything and nothing at all.

The apothecary smelled of cloves, with a sharp undercurrent of something acrid, like scorched herbs. It was early enough that the streets were empty, but the shop was open, lanterns glowing behind the latticed windows.

Nell pushed open the door with more force than necessary. The bell overhead gave a startled jangle.

Mei Ling looked up from the back counter, where she was grinding something dark and oily in a brass mortar. Her sleeves were rolled to the elbow, her hands calm and steady. Unlike Nell, Mei never seemed rattled, never lost control.

"You're early," she said, her voice neutral but her dark eyes sharp, assessing.

"I didn't think I'd make it at all," Nell replied, shutting the door behind her and bolting it. She didn't want interruptions. Not now. "Is anyone else here?"

"Just us," Mei said, setting aside her work and wiping her hands on a cloth. "I sent Xiu to the market."

Mei studied her for a beat, taking in Nell's disheveled appearance, the dark circles beneath her eyes. "Something's happened."

Nell crossed the shop in three strides, stopped short at the counter, and met her friend's eyes. "We're being targeted. A rival smuggler, Thomas Thorne, do you know the name?"

Mei nodded. "Unfortunately."

"They're planning to seize the next shipment. Sabotage it. Or us. And my crew, what's left of them, they're frightened. I can't protect them. I can't protect anything."

Her voice cracked on the last word, and she blinked rapidly to hold back the hot pressure of tears. She'd cried in front of Elijah last night; she wouldn't break down again so soon.

Mei set down the pestle. "So now you see what I meant."

"What do I do?" Nell asked, voice low, fierce with desperation. "Jonny will say he can fix it with blood. But I— I can't do this anymore."

Mei gestured for her to sit on the low stool by the counter. Nell obeyed, her limbs trembling now that she had stopped moving.

Her face was carefully neutral, but her eyes were kind in a way few people ever saw. "You disappear."

Nell looked up, startled, certain she'd misheard.

"You burn the warehouse," Mei said, as if suggesting nothing more dramatic than closing a ledger. "Say it was another dock fire. No survivors found. You vanish." She made a fluid gesture with one elegant hand. "No one questions what's already in ashes."

Nell stared at her, horrified. "You're serious?" The words came out in a strangled whisper. "Fake my own death?!"

"Of course." Mei's expression didn't change. "You can't keep running this operation, not with rivals like Thorne on your heels and the police closing in. You think Jonny can fight off everyone? Even he has limits." She paused. "And even if he could, is that who you want to be? The woman who lets men get beaten half to death to protect her business?"

"I can't give up the business," Nell whispered, hands twisting in the fabric of her skirt. "It's my father's legacy, all I have left of him."

"Your father is gone," Mei said gently but firmly. "And the man he was would not want this for you. Would not want you afraid, compromised, losing your soul piece by piece."

Nell looked away, swallowing the lump in her throat. She knew Mei was right. The father she'd idolized wouldn't recognize what she'd become in her desperate attempts to save what he'd built.

"You could start again," Mei said, softer now. She reached across the counter to touch Nell's hand, her fingers warm and steady. "Somewhere else. Another city. The continent, perhaps. With a new name. You're smart enough. You have money hidden away, don't deny it, I know you do. I have connections. I can help you disappear."

Nell's voice wavered. "And never see Elijah again?"

Mei didn't answer.

That silence was more brutal than any reply.

Nell pressed her fists into her lap, trying to hold herself together. She'd fought too hard, risked too much, to end it all in smoke. But staying might kill her. Or someone she loved.

"You have to choose," Mei said. "Power or freedom. You can't have both."

Nell watched her friend's hands move in their steady rhythm, envying her certainty, her clarity. She'd been balancing on the edge for too long. It was time to choose which way to fall.

The warehouse office was cloaked in half-light, the single gas lamp casting long shadows against the walls. Nell stepped inside, her shoulders tight with the weight of what Mei had said. *You burn the warehouse. Say it was another dock fire. No survivors found. You vanish.* The thought of walking away, burning everything down, felt like death itself. The end of everything she'd fought for. And yet, wasn't that what this had become? A slow death by a thousand compromises?

She hadn't taken more than two steps before she realised she wasn't alone.

Jonny stood by the window, the flame from his match catching briefly on the edge of his grin as he lit a cigarette.

"Evening, my lady," he said, smoke curling from his lips like a serpent. "Didn't expect you back here at this time of night. Thought you'd be tucked away in that fancy Islington house of yours."

Nell didn't let her surprise show. She'd learned that much at least. Never give Jonny the satisfaction of catching her off guard. She removed her gloves deliberately, one finger at a time.

"I had some things to think about," she said, keeping her voice neutral.

"About Thomas Thorne, I'd wager." He took another drag, the ember of his cigarette glowing orange in the dimness. Not a question. A statement.

Her spine stiffened. "So the rumours are true?"

"Oh, he's sniffing around. Sent one of his lads to ask questions about your manifests. Real subtle, that lot."

He took another long drag and watched her carefully, smoke veiling his expression. "We should deal with it before it gets messy. Before he gets bold."

"And by 'deal with it,' I assume you don't mean send a letter."

Jonny chuckled. "Letters are for people who care about paper trails and propriety. I'm talking about sending a message, the kind people remember."

Nell didn't reply right away. She crossed to the desk and pretended to shuffle through the ledgers, anything to avoid the intensity of his gaze. Her father's fountain pen lay where she'd left it that morning, the gold nib catching the lamplight. What would he think of her now? Of the choices she was weighing?

"I can handle Thorne," Jonny went on, stepping closer. "You've got enough to worry about keeping the business afloat. Let me take care of the dirt."

She glanced up, studying his face. There was something almost tender in his expression, a protectiveness that might have been touching if it weren't so dangerous. "And what will it cost me?" she asked quietly.

His grin widened. "Nothing more than what you're already giving. Trust. The belief that we're on the same side."

Nell swallowed hard. "And you're sure this is the only way?"

"You want to keep this business? Keep your

name, your routes, your standing?" Jonny spread his hands, palms up, as if the answer were obvious. "Then yes. In this world, our world, you need someone willing to get their hands dirty so yours stay clean." His eyes never left hers, intense and unwavering.

He leaned against the desk, his voice dropping an octave. "You've done the hard part, Nell. You built something. You built something from the wreckage your father left behind. You command respect down here. Even the old salts who wouldn't give a woman the time of day now tip their caps when you walk by. All you need now is someone to keep the wolves at bay."

She met his gaze, and for a moment, she felt that old thrill again. The pull of danger, the promise of control, the temptation of someone who would burn down the world for her.

"You don't have to run from any of this," he said, reading the conflict in her eyes with unnerving accuracy. "Not when you could own it. Build it higher. Make them all remember your name."

Nell smiled, carefully measured. "Thank you, Jonny. I appreciate your loyalty."

He studied her for a long moment, as if trying to read beneath the surface, then tipped an imaginary hat and pushed off the desk. "Just say the word, love. One nod from you, and Thorne disappears." He took a final drag of his cigarette before crushing it beneath his heel. "Sleep on it. I'll be around."

When he was gone, she stood very still in the silence.

In Jonny's eyes, she was still the Queen of the Docks, untouchable and fierce. Was that a position she should give up lightly? For all his brutality, he offered a certainty Elijah couldn't. The promise that she could keep her father's legacy intact, that she wouldn't have to disappear into some anonymous new life, starting from nothing.

Maybe Mei was wrong. If Jonny could get rid of this final threat from Thomas Thorne, things could be smooth sailing again. The business could thrive. Her father's name would live on through her. And wasn't that what she'd wanted all along?

Elijah or Jonny. Flight or fight. The woman she was or the woman she might become.

The gas lamp flickered, shadows dancing across the walls. What kind of queen did she truly want to be?

Over at the station house on Cable Street it was unusually quiet for a Thursday evening. Rain tapped steadily against the windows. Inspector Elijah Hart sat hunched at his desk, busying himself with the overflow of reports from his in-tray.

A knock at the door announced Constable Peters. He had papers tucked beneath one arm and a file clutched in the other, knuckles white with what might have been nervousness.

"Sir, sorry to interrupt," Peters said, his voice carrying a slight tremor, "but something's come in from the Thames checkpoint. Customs flagged a crate shipment that didn't match the declared cargo list. They're asking for immediate attention."

Elijah looked up, eyes narrowing slightly beneath heavy brows. "Where?"

"Warehouse 14, Limehouse Basin. Warrington & Company."

His spine stiffened, and something cold slithered down his back. Warrington's—Nell's business. The business her father had built from nothing. The same business whose ledgers she'd grown increasingly reluctant to discuss.

"What was inside?" he asked, his voice betraying nothing of the storm brewing beneath.

Peters flipped open the file, the pages rustling in the quiet room. "Markings matched those linked to an opium ring operating out of Canton. Small traces confirmed it, high grade, from what the inspectors could tell. Hidden beneath bolts of silk fabric and lighting fixtures."

Elijah reached out and took the file with steady hands that belied the tremor in his chest. His eyes scanned the customs report, the crate's tracking number, the declaration forged under his own department's nose. A cold sweat broke out across his forehead as his gaze dropped to the signature line.

Thomas Finch, one of Nell's dock managers. And above that, scrawled in a rushed but unmistakable hand, her initials. EW. Eleanor Warrington.

A heavy silence settled between the two men. Peters, clearly uncomfortable with the weight of it, cleared his throat. "There's a recommendation from the customs office, sir. They want to open a formal investigation. Proper paperwork. Interviews. Could be high profile, given the... connections."

Elijah nodded slowly, his face a careful blank. "Thank you, Constable. I'll handle this personally. Not a word to anyone else, understood?"

"Yes, sir," Peters replied, relief evident in his voice as he backed toward the door. "Good night, Inspector."

When the door clicked shut, Elijah dropped his head into his hands. He laid the report on the desk before him and simply stared, the words blurring together.

Nell.

There had been doubts. Whispers in certain circles that a woman couldn't run a shipping company without cutting corners. He'd attributed it to the pressures of business, the weight of being a woman in a man's world. But this was proof. Cold, ugly proof that the whispers had merit.

She hadn't denied anything. She'd cried in his arms, her tears soaking through his shirt. Said it had started small and grown out of control. That she was trapped now, in too deep.

And now he knew why.

He rested his elbows on the desk and pressed his fingers to his mouth, feeling the rough scratch of day-old stubble. His chest felt hollow, his heartbeat a dull, aching thud behind his ribs.

He desperately wanted to believe it was a mistake. That someone had planted the crates. That she had been set up by rivals. That she hadn't known the true nature of what her ships carried.

But he knew her, her meticulous attention to detail. Knew how she examined every invoice, supervised every major shipment personally. No detail escaped her notice. It was how she'd survived in this cutthroat business.

She had known. And still, she'd let him kiss her like he was the only good thing left in her life.

He picked up the report again, holding it as if it weighed more than paper ever could.

Then, softly, almost inaudibly, he whispered, "Nell... what have you done?"

The gas lamp hissed softly in the silence, casting long shadows across the walls.

Outside, the rain turned heavier, drumming against the windows with increasing urgency, as if warning of a coming storm.

And Elijah knew that whatever line had once existed between his heart and his badge—that fragile boundary he'd maintained with such care—was gone.

CHAPTER 15

The knock echoed through the drafty house like a gunshot, sharp and final.

Nell flinched where she sat in the lounge's faded armchair, a half-empty teacup forgotten on the side table beside her. She had been waiting for this moment since dawn, perhaps expecting it even, when the morning's silence had stretched too long and the air around the warehouse had begun to feel watchful again. The sidelong glances from her men had become unbearable. Some concerned, others suspicious, until she'd sought refuge in the hollow comfort of home.

She moved to the door with leaden steps, her fingers hesitating on the latch before drawing it open slowly.

Elijah stood on the threshold, rain glistening on his broad shoulders and dampening his dark hair. His jaw was clenched tight, his eyes darker still—not with anger, she realized with a pang, but with disappointment. That was infinitely worse.

"May I come in?" His voice was carefully controlled, professional.

She stepped back wordlessly and gestured to the sitting room beyond.

The door closed behind them with a soft click. He didn't remove his rain-spotted coat. Didn't accept the seat she didn't offer. Didn't speak for a long moment that stretched between them like an accusation.

Nell braced herself, squaring her shoulders. "Elijah—"

"No," he said sharply, cutting through her words before they could form into the excuses she'd been rehearsing. "Before you talk yourself into more lies, I need you to listen."

He reached into the inner pocket of his coat and pulled out a bundle of documents, bound with twine. He tossed them onto the seat beside her.

"There's a witness," he said. "A dockhand. Said he saw you reviewing the crates before customs got there. Said you gave specific instructions to keep one of them off the manifest. There's a signature on the shipping order. Yours. And there's more. Crates relabelled, contents misdeclared."

Nell didn't look down at the papers. She didn't need to. She'd seen every one of them before, some with her own ink still drying on the margins.

Her silence hung in the air, an admission more damning than any confession.

Elijah's jaw tightened. "I needed it to be wrong. I needed someone to have framed you." His shoulders sagged slightly. "But you did this."

Still she said nothing, her throat too tight for words.

He stepped forward, placing both hands on her shoulders gently, leaning in. "Do you know what that means, Nell? What you've involved yourself in?"

His voice cracked. "I trusted you."

Nell swallowed. "I didn't ask for your trust."

"But you took it," he snapped, fingers tightening briefly on her shoulders before he released her. "You let me believe, God, you let me believe you were better than all this. That you were different."

She finally met his eyes. There was no anger in hers. Only exhaustion.

"You came here to arrest me?" It wasn't really a question.

"I should," he said. "I should have, the moment I walked through the door."

They stood in silence, the only sound the faint ticking of the wall clock. Elijah straightened slowly, putting distance between them as though proximity to her clouded his judgment.

"I need you to tell me something," he said finally. "And I want the truth, Nell. No more half-truths. No more evasions.

Nell nodded once.

"Why?" he asked. "Why all of this?"

And then her voice broke.

"I only ever wanted to do right by the widowed families," she said, barely more than a whisper.

"After the shipwreck... they lost everything. Husbands, sons, brothers, and then their livelihoods too. The money from the company wasn't coming. The insurance was declared void. I had to find something, anything, to keep them fed. And then it got out of hand. And then it was too late."

Elijah's eyes closed for half a second, as though the weight of her words had struck him.

When he opened them again, she saw it: the war inside him.

Love and law. Justice and mercy. Duty and heartbreak.

He didn't speak.

He didn't need to.

Nell turned away from him, arms folded tightly across her chest, her breath shallow.

Elijah stayed where he was, but his gaze followed her like a shadow. When he spoke again, his voice was quieter, more measured. But no less sharp.

"I didn't come here just because of the smuggling."

She looked up warily.

He reached into his coat once more and produced another folded paper, this one smudged with soot at the corners. He laid it on the desk beside the others.

"You remember the fire? The one that damaged your warehouse? You told me you thought it was a rival. Thomas Thorne. So did I."

He paused. "But it wasn't."

Nell frowned, genuine confusion crossing her features. "What do you mean?"

"I traced the pattern," he said. "There's been a string of incidents. Fires, stolen crates, intimidation tactics, all tied to cargo yards used by Warrington & Co. And also the same calling card left at all the incidents. The Jack of Hearts"

She blinked, slowly, remembering the same card being left at the first warehouse fire. "So?"

Elijah's eyes darkened. "So I looked deeper. And do you know whose name kept coming up? Quietly, but often enough to raise flags?"

A long pause.

"Jonny Collins."

Nell didn't speak. Couldn't.

"He's the one spreading Thorne's name as a cover. He's the one staging the threats. Even the crate tampering. It all started once you began working with him. He's been orchestrating it for months." Elijah's hands clenched at his sides. "Just enough chaos to make you scared. Just enough damage to seem credible. And just enough protection to make you trust him."

Elijah stepped toward her, his expression softening slightly. "He wanted you reliant. Afraid. Dependent on his muscle, his connections, his promises of safety."

"No," she whispered, shaking her head. "No. That doesn't make sense. He helped me. He warned me about threats. He—"

"—made himself indispensable," Elijah finished grimly. "That's how control works, Nell. Create the sickness, then sell the cure."

She sank into the nearest chair, as though her knees had given way beneath her. The reality of it, the elaborate trap she'd walked into, crashed over her in waves.

"I thought..." she began, then stopped. There were too many thoughts colliding in her mind, none of them coherent. "I thought he was helping me survive."

Elijah's voice was gentler now, tinged with something like pity. "He was helping you survive a trap he laid himself."

Nell looked at him, wide-eyed and wounded. "Why would he do that? What does he gain?"

"Because power's like opium to men like him," he said, crouching before her chair to meet her gaze directly. "They don't just want a cut of your business or your profits. They want to own you. They want to be the hand that feeds and the hand that strikes. They want you grateful for scraps of what was yours to begin with."

She covered her face with both hands, shoulders curving inward.

"I'm such a fool," she whispered between her fingers.

"No," he said quietly, reaching up to pull her

hands gently away from her face. "You're not. You were trying to save what mattered to you. People who had no one else. He just... knew exactly how to twist that goodness into something he could use."

A silence passed between them, heavy with unspoken possibilities and regrets.

"And now?" she asked finally, her voice cracking on the question. "What happens now, Elijah?"

Elijah's expression hardened. "Now, Nell... you have a choice. Maybe you can tell the truth, unless you've forgotten how."

The silence in the room grew heavy, like fog pressing in from every corner. Outside, the rain intensified, drumming against the windows in an uneven rhythm.

Nell sat, her shoulders slumped, hands trembling in her lap. She stared at them—once steady hands that had confidently signed manifests, counted coin, and shaken on deals. Now they betrayed her, quivering like autumn leaves. The last of her composure was crumbling, flaking away like ash.

"I never meant for this to happen," she said, her voice cracked. "I didn't wake up one day and decide to smuggle opium."

Elijah said nothing. He had moved to the

window, one hand braced against the frame, watching raindrops chase each other down the glass. His silence was not merciful; it was a demand for more. He simply waited.

She forced herself to keep going, to let it all pour out.

"When the Eleanor went down and the money from the insurers didn't come... I watched those widows come to my door, begging to help me fill their empty pantries. I saw their children, holloweyed and threadbare. And all I could think was, 'If I don't do something, they'll starve. And it'll be on me.'"

She met his eyes, the weight of her shame laid bare. No artifice remained, only the naked truth she'd hidden for so long.

"I only ever wanted to do right by them. To carry on what my father built. To make him proud. But I couldn't make the numbers work. I couldn't keep the crews paid. I was drowning."

She swallowed hard.

"And then someone made me an offer, not directly. But they left the door open. And I walked through it. I told myself it was one shipment. Then another. Then it was too late. There were debts I couldn't untangle. Lies I couldn't unwind." She glanced up but Elijah was still studying the window pane.

"Jonny promised protection. He made me feel like I still had control, like I still had a choice." A bitter smile crossed her face. "But every step led further into something I didn't recognise. The business my father built became... something else. And so did I."

She laughed bitterly. "You want the truth, Elijah? I don't even know who I am anymore."

He crossed to the centre of the room, rigid, his face unreadable.

"I should arrest you," he said finally. His voice wasn't angry. It was hollow.

"I know." She couldn't bear to hear the disappointment in his words. Not from Elijah, who had once looked at her with such warmth, who'd once thought so much of her.

"You've committed a serious crime. Multiple crimes. You've lied to customs officials, to your own workers." His voice hardened slightly. "You've endangered lives with those shipments. Opium that ends up in the desperate hands of the poor, in the dens down by the river. Maybe been responsible for a life or two being lost in those dark places."

"I know."

"And worst of all," he added, voice barely above a whisper, "you lied to me."

It landed like a gut punch.

Nell blinked hard against the tears gathering behind her eyes, determined not to let them fall. "I didn't lie to you. Not really." Even to her own ears, the words sounded pathetic. "I just... couldn't tell you the truth."

"That's worse."

He turned away, running a hand through his damp hair. His silhouette against the lamplight looked older somehow. Worn down by the weight of too many compromises, too many disappointments.

She didn't plead. Didn't beg for understanding or forgiveness. She knew she'd already used up every ounce of his faith in her. Every shred of the benefit of doubt he'd so generously extended.

He stood there for a long time.

Then, quietly, he said, "You should pack a bag."

She looked up sharply. "What?"

"You need to disappear. Tonight. If I stay here much longer, I'll have no choice but to turn you in. My duty will override..." He trailed off, unwilling to name what lay between them.

"Elijah—" She stood, taking a hesitant step toward him.

"I can't help you again, Nell," he said, turning back to face her. His eyes were shining. "I've already compromised too much. This is where we part ways."

Those words—so final, so absolute—made her chest constrict painfully.

She took another step forward, her voice trembling. "Is this really goodbye?"

He didn't answer right away. Then he stepped toward her, took her face in his hands, and for a moment, he simply looked at her, as though committing every detail to memory.

And then he kissed her once, softly, like a memory being made. Like a door being closed.

When he pulled away, she was crying, silent tears tracking down her cheeks and over his fingers.

"I never stopped believing in the girl I met on the docks," he said. "But I don't know if she's still in there."

She nodded, unable to speak.

And then he was gone, moving away from her with painful finality. His footsteps echoed in the hallway, hesitated briefly at the door, a moment of doubt, perhaps, or simply reluctance, and then continued.

The door clicked shut behind him.

Nell stood in the silence that followed, the weight of her choices settling in like stone. She remained there long after the rain had slowed to a drizzle, after the fire had died completely in the grate.

CHAPTER 16

The next morning, Nell awoke with a start in the armchair where she had spent the night, her neck stiff and a dull ache throbbing behind her eyes. She had no memory of falling asleep—only of staring into the fire until the flames had dulled to ember, then ash, marking the hours with their slow decay.

Dawn had come despite everything, casting a soft, unforgiving glow over the parlor and, with it, the cold reality of all that had transpired the night before.

For a fleeting moment, everything felt still—normal, even. The familiar weight of the house settled around her like an old blanket. Through the window, she could see the cherry tree in the garden, its branches heavy with spring blossoms.

But the illusion shattered almost instantly as the events of the previous night came rushing back. Elijah standing in the rain, the documents in his hands, his voice breaking as he spoke of betrayal and duty and lost trust. The crushing weight of it all returned, settling heavily in her chest until each breath felt labored.

"I can't help you again, Nell." The echo of his words seemed to hang in the air still.

Elijah had given her a choice when he walked out of the house, his heart in pieces. But was it ever truly a choice?

She understood the truth of it with brutal clarity now—if she stayed, he would have no option but to do his duty. And she wasn't sure she had the strength for what would follow: the public humiliation of arrest, the harsh conditions of a women's prison, the scandal that would destroy what remained of her father's legacy... or for seeing the disappointment in Elijah's eyes once more as he testified against her. That, perhaps, would be the cruelest punishment of all.

Though she'd turned it over endlessly in her mind throughout the long night, examining it from every angle, the answer had always been the same. There was no other course left to her but to vanish.

With a heavy sigh, she pushed herself up from the chair. The room tilted briefly before steadying itself. When had she last eaten? She couldn't remember.

She climbed the stairs slowly, one hand trailing along the wall for support, each step feeling as though she carried the weight of the house itself on her shoulders. The floorboards creaked beneath her feet—familiar sounds that she had known since childhood. How strange to think she might never hear them again.

She dressed in the plainest clothes she owned, garments meant not to draw attention.

Standing before the mirror, she pinned her hair into a neat coil, smoothing the unruly tendrils at her temples. The woman who stared back at her from the looking glass seemed like a stranger—older than she remembered, worn and hollow-eyed, with a quiet sorrow set deep into her features and new lines etched at the corners of her mouth. When had those appeared?

It was time. The morning would not wait for her regrets or second thoughts.

Descending the staircase in silence, her hand

brushed lightly along the banister. Every object in the house suddenly seemed precious, laden with memories she would soon have to leave behind.

The grandfather clock in the parlour ticked steadily, each chime echoing louder in the hush of the house. Outside, the city had begun to stir—the distant rattle of cart wheels, the clatter of hooves, the muffled cries of costermongers calling their wares. Life continuing, heedless of her private collapse.

But inside, her world was still. Suspended between what had been and what must come next.

She passed into the drawing room, now bathed in morning light, and let her eyes rest briefly on the wingback armchair where her father had once sat reading his newspaper, pipe smoke curling above his head while he muttered about shipping routes and customs regulations. How disappointed he would be to see what had become of his daughter and his business. Or would he understand, perhaps better than anyone, the impossible choices she had faced?

She could scarcely believe she was about to leave it all behind.

But she couldn't dwell on that now. Not now.

Once more, perhaps for the last time, she would have to ask Mei Ling for help.

The familiar tinkle of the bell echoed softly as

Nell stepped into Mei Ling's apothecary, the sound both comforting and jarring in her fragile state. The morning light filtered through cloth-covered windows, casting the interior in a warm glow that seemed at odds with the turmoil in Nell's heart.

Behind the narrow counter, Mei barely looked up from the herbs she was grinding, as though she'd been expecting this particular visitor at this particular hour.

"There's been trouble?" Mei asked, finally raising her eyes to study Nell, who looked almost unrecognisable with her hunched posture, red-rimmed eyes, and the absence of the confident bearing that had always defined her. The question was rhetorical

Nell fought to hold her composure.

"It's over, Mei," she said quietly, her voice roughened from a night of unshed tears. "Elijah knows everything."

The pestle in Mei's hand paused mid-grind, then resumed for two more deliberate rotations before she set it down with careful precision beside the stone mortar.

"How much does he know?" she asked, voice low and steady. "Do I need to alert my team?"

Nell shook her head. "No... he doesn't know about *your* involvement. He only has proof of mine.

My name on the manifests. A statement from one of my dockhands. He gave me an ultimatum."

Her voice cracked on the last word, and she blinked rapidly to hold back the tears that threatened to spill over. She would not weep here, in the open shop where anyone might enter. She had that much dignity left, at least.

"I see," Mei said calmly, her dark eyes revealing nothing of her thoughts. She reached out and touched Nell's elbow with light fingers. "Come through to the back room. We have much to discuss, and these walls", she glanced meaningfully at the thin partition separating the shop from the street, "have always been too eager to share their secrets."

She took Nell gently by the elbow and guided her through. Nell couldn't help but notice how composed Mei remained. Calm, controlled, as though chaos had no power over her realm. Nell wondered, bitterly, why she hadn't been able to do the same. Why her world was unraveling while Mei stood unaffected as ever, like a stone in a rushing river.

The back room was small but neatly arranged, with a low table surrounded by cushions, a cast-iron stove in the corner, and shelves containing books in both English and Chinese. A painted screen depicted herons standing in misty water, their long necks arched in eternal vigilance.

"Sit there," Mei instructed as she busied herself at the little stove. "I'm going to make you some mint tea. It will settle your nerves. Now—tell me exactly what Inspector Hart said."

"He gave me a choice," Nell whispered. "Though it's not much of one. Either I disappear—today—or I stay, and he'll have no choice but to arrest me."

Mei nodded slowly, unblinking, as she measured dried mint leaves into a small clay teapot. Her movements were precise, almost ritualistic. "I see."

There was a pause filled only with the gentle bubble of water coming to boil. Mei seemed to be calculating something, weighing options Nell couldn't begin to fathom.

"And Johnny?" she asked finally, her tone unreadable as she poured steaming water over the leaves. The sharp, clean scent of mint filled the small room. "Does he know about your... situation?"

Nell looked up sharply. She hadn't even thought of him.

"I... I don't think he knows," she said. "Not yet."

"Good," said Mai. "Then we still have time."

Nell looked up sharply. In her distress over Elijah, she hadn't even thought of Johnny Collins and what his reaction might be when he discovered she could no longer be useful to him. That she could no longer provide the access and respectability his operation needed.

"I... I don't think he knows," she said, a new fear blooming in her chest. "Not yet."

"Good," said Mei, the slightest hint of relief in her voice. "Then we still have time."

She placed a small cup of tea before Nell, the liquid pale green and fragrant. Nell stared at her, searching that composed face for some explanation.

"You have a plan?" she asked, hope flickering to life for the first time since Elijah had walked out of her door.

"Of course," Mei replied smoothly. "In this line of work, there always needs to be a plan. A contingency for when things inevitably go wrong. But you're not going to like it."

Nell sighed, picking up the teacup and letting its warmth seep into her cold fingers. She felt weary beyond words, hollowed out by regret. "There's very little about this situation I do like. What could possibly be worse than what I'm already facing?"

"What I am about to suggest is... extreme. But it is the only way to ensure your complete freedom from both the law and from Johnny Collins."

Nell's stomach tightened with apprehension. "Go on."

Mei took a breath, studying Nell's face as though gauging whether she could bear what was to come. "Very well, then. Listen carefully. You must go to the docks as normal today," Mei began, her voice steady. "Act as you would on any other day. Show your face. Be seen by your workers, by the other merchants. By anyone who might later be questioned."

Nell nodded slowly, though confusion creased her brow. "But why? If I need to disappear—"

Mei held up one delicate hand, silencing her. "Are there any shipments arriving today?"

Nell shook her head. "No. The Perseverance isn't due from Calcutta for another three days, and the smaller vessels are all out."

"Good. That simplifies matters." Mei leaned forward slightly, her voice dropping even lower. "This evening, I want you to make sure every worker has gone home. Give them an extra half-day's wages if you must. The warehouse must be completely empty. No one can remain behind, do you understand?"

Nell frowned. "And then?"

"Then," Mei continued, her dark eyes holding Nell's with unwavering intensity, "you'll bring the clothes you wore that day here, along with something identifiable. A brooch. A ring. That distinctive pearl hairpin your father brought back from Paris. Anything unmistakably yours that could survive... intense heat."

Nell's brow creased deeper, her mind racing to catch up with the implications of Mei's words. "Why would I need—"

And then understanding dawned, cold and horrifying.

"You'll wait here during the night," Mei went on, confirming Nell's suspicion. "You'll be safe. No one will think to look for you here. And before dawn..." She paused, watching Nell closely. "The warehouse will burn to the ground. A terrible accident. And among the ashes, they will find a body—dressed in your clothes, wearing your jewellery, too badly damaged for proper identification, but with enough evidence to convince the authorities."

Nell gasped, her hand flying to her mouth. "No. That's—that's monstrous. I can't—"

""It's the only way," Mei said, her voice calm but firm. She reached out and steadied Nell's hand before the tea could spill. "Think, Eleanor. If you simply disappear, what happens? The police search for you. Johnny searches for you. Your assets are frozen but not released. Those widows you care so much about remain in limbo, with no resolution. But if you are believed dead..."

Nell set the cup down with shaking hands, her stomach churning. "But... whose body?" she whispered, horrified at the thought. "You can't mean to kill someone just to—"

"Don't concern yourself," Mei replied, a shadow passing over her features. "I have connections at the morgue. There are always unclaimed bodies. Those who died alone, with no family to mourn them. It will be handled."

Nell's stomach turned violently. The mint tea that had been so soothing moments before now threatened to come back up. Her hands trembled in her lap. "I can't believe it's come to this. To such... such deception."

"If you want people like Johnny Collins off your back for good, Nell, this is the only way." Mei's voice hardened slightly. "If he thinks you've vanished, gone into hiding, he'll never stop hunting you. He'll see it as a betrayal, an insult. But if he thinks you're dead..."

Mei let the words hang in the air between them.

"He'll have no reason to pursue you," she finished softly. "No reason to question."

Nell stared at her, searching that composed face

for any sign of doubt or hesitation. She found none. Only cool certainty.

"But where will I go? What will I do?" Nell's voice was barely above a whisper. "I have no identity beyond Eleanor Warrington. No skills beyond what my father taught me. I don't know how to be anyone else."

"I'll have new documents waiting for you here," Mei said. "A birth certificate. Travel permits. Letters of introduction. Bank drafts that cannot be traced. Everything you'll need to start again."

"But... how?" Nell asked, bewildered by the complexity of what Mei proposed. "Such documents take time to create. Connections. Money."

"A friend is helping," Mei said simply, her expression revealing nothing. "No one you know."

Nell studied her closely, suspicion flaring. In her world, help always came with strings attached, with debts to be repaid. "Are you sure? Are you certain it's no one connected to Johnny? Or to any of the other operations at the docks?"

Mei's eyes flickered momentarily, the only break in her perfect composure. "Family," she said. "No one you know. But someone who owes me."

She reached across the table, her tone softening. "This is your only chance, Nell. You get to walk away. Start again. Leave behind the mess—leave behind *him*."

Nell exhaled shakily and wiped her tears with the back of her hand. "Could I ever come back?" she asked, though she already knew the answer.

Mei shook her head once, definitively. "The dead do not return, Nell. Not if they wish to remain safe."

The finality of it struck Nell like a physical blow. Never to see London again. Never to walk along the docks where she had grown up. Never to see Elijah, even from afar.

But what alternative did she have? Prison? Disgrace? Or worse, whatever vengeance Johnny Collins might extract when he discovered she could no longer be useful to him?

"Very well," she whispered. "I'll do it."

Mei nodded, satisfaction flickering briefly across her features. "You should go. Head to the docks as usual—we don't want to arouse suspicion. Act normally. Speak to your workers. Be seen."

Nell rose from her chair, her knees unsteady.

"And tomorrow?" she asked, her voice catching. "What happens after the fire?"

"Tomorrow," Mei said, "you'll be someone else."

CHAPTER 17

The morning mist clung low over the docks, veiling everything in a hush that made the world feel quieter than it should. Nell arrived early, her breath clouding in the brittle air. The weight in her chest was almost a comfort now, an old friend she no longer tried to push away.

Her office door creaked open. She stepped inside and hung up her coat with care, smoothing the lapels as if the neatness of it might somehow anchor her to the moment, to this life that was slipping through her fingers. But it was no use. Every tick of the clock on the wall echoed with the knowledge that by tonight, she would no longer be Nell Warrington.

Through the window, she watched the men loading crates onto the carts, their movements efficient and familiar. She knew every one of them by name: Tomlinson with his bad knee, Carter who never removed his cap even indoors, young Frank who'd only just stopped calling her "Miss Nell" and blushing when she addressed him directly. She tried not to think of how they would react when the news came. How many would be upset. How many would think it was for the best.

Her hands itched to be busy. She moved to the desk, shuffled a few manifest sheets, adjusted the inkwell, even straightened the blotter. Anything to stop her mind drifting back to Elijah. To his voice. The hurt in his eyes when he'd said goodbye.

It hurt more than she expected, that he'd meant it.

The kettle on the small iron stove rattled with heat. She poured herself a cup of tea but didn't drink it. She stared down at the swirling surface, watching it grow still.

This was her last morning here. After today, she would vanish. A sound snapped her out of her reverie.

She heard him before she saw him—the distinctive rhythm of his boots on the wooden floorboards, the lazy creak of the office door swinging open without invitation.

Jonny leaned against the frame, arms folded, his coat collar still damp from the morning mist. That familiar grin played on his lips, but his eyes were sharper today, more watchful.

"Well, don't you look like a woman with the weight of the Empire on her shoulders," he drawled. "Rough morning?"

Nell glanced up from her paperwork, feigning calm. "Just tired. It's been a long week."

He stepped inside, letting the door fall shut behind him. "Thought you'd be celebrating. That last shipment went through like butter. Not a customs man in sight." His smile widened. "Almost like someone greased the right palms beforehand."

Her pen hovered mid-line on the ledger, a tiny betrayal she hoped he hadn't noticed. "Plenty more to do. Success is fleeting in this business."

Jonny tilted his head, studying her like a puzzle he was determined to solve. "Funny, you've been twitchier than a cat in a doghouse since Tuesday. Everything all right?"

"I said I'm fine." Her voice was light, almost breezy. "Just pressure. You know how it is."

"I'll bet," he said, moving further into the room, running a finger along the edge of her desk. "Only, pressure doesn't usually make you look like you're packing for a one-way trip to the moon."

She stiffened, just slightly. "Don't be ridiculous."

He offered a thin smile. "Wouldn't dream of it."

A silence passed between them.

"Have you heard anything else about Thorne?" she asked, flipping a page in the ledger as if the question were an afterthought. "Some of the men are spooked."

Jonny didn't answer immediately. His hesitation lasted a beat too long. "Yeah... word is he's moving in heavier. Few more warehouses burned down Millwall way. Two men found floating face-down by the ferry crossing. Nasty bugger, Thorne."

Nell looked up, meeting his gaze directly. "I thought you said he operated out of Whitechapel?"

Jonny blinked. "I did. I mean, he does. Usually." His fingers drummed once against the desk. "But he's expanding now, apparently. Always sniffing for weakness.

There it was—the stumble. The hesitation. Elijah had told her something different. Something cleaner. And Jonny had just muddied it.

Her pulse quickened.

But she didn't flinch.

Instead, she gave a soft sigh. "It's hard to know

what's real these days. Who to trust."

His shoulders stiffened. "What's that supposed to mean?"

"Nothing." She shook her head quickly, too quickly. "Just tired, like I said. The docks feel full of shadows lately, that's all. Rumours everywhere. It's hard to sort through them."

Jonny studied her in silence for a moment too long.

Then he crossed to her, slowly, and reached out. His fingers brushed her jaw, trailing lightly down to her collarbone. The touch was unexpectedly tender, possessive in a way that made her throat tighten.

"You and me," he said, voice low. "We've always been a team. Don't forget that, Nell."

She managed a small smile. "I won't."

He stepped back, eyes lingering on her face as if memorizing it, or perhaps searching for cracks in her façade.

"I'll be in touch. Don't go anywhere." He winked at her.

And then he was gone, the door closing behind him with a soft click that sounded to Nell like a trap springing shut.

Only when she could no longer hear his footsteps did she finally release the breath she'd been holding.

It escaped in a ragged exhale, her shoulders collapsing inward as though the tension that had braced her spine all morning had finally given out.

Her palms were damp with cold sweat. She wiped them against her skirt, once, twice, leaving faint marks on the fabric. A small tell that would have given her away if Jonny had still been there to see it. She'd grown careless.

She turned toward the filing cabinet in the corner, where she'd stashed the bundle of clothes that she needed to take to Mei. With the package in hand, she turned back to her desk.

It was tidy. Purposefully so. She'd cleared it the evening before, as if that might make leaving easier. It hadn't.

She looked around the room one final time.

The scuffed desk, the crooked shelf of ledgers, the half-worn path in the floorboards where her boots had paced through so many sleepless evenings. All of it hers. All of it about to be smoke.

She turned off the lamp, pulled on her gloves, and lifted the parcel beneath her arm.

Then, without another glance, her chin lifted with a defiance that no one was there to witness, she walked out of the office and closed the door behind her—this time, for good.

Outside, the docks were quieter now. The morning's bustle had given way to the lull before evening shifts. She kept her pace measured, neither too hurried nor too leisurely. Someone in a rush drew attention. Someone dawdling invited questions. She moved with purpose. Three streets down, she paused at the corner and glanced back. No one there

The sun was sinking low behind the chimneys when Nell turned the final corner into the narrow street where the apothecary sat. The mist that had hovered over the city all morning had thinned now, giving way to a washed-out sky tinged with the orange blush of approaching dusk.

She paused, scanning the street. A woman with a basket. An old man smoking a pipe on a doorstep. A stray cat slinking along a fence. Nothing unusual. Nothing that set her nerves jangling.

She stepped into the apothecary with barely a sound. The doorbell gave a faint chime, more delicate than usual, as if even it understood the need for silence.

Mei was waiting.

She stood behind the counter, sleeves rolled to her elbows, a fine layer of ash smudging one wrist. Her dark eyes, keen as a hawk's, took in Nell's appearance in one swift assessment. She didn't speak, didn't offer a greeting. She merely held Nell's gaze for a long, measured moment, and then gave a single, short nod.

"You weren't followed?" Mei asked, her voice barely above a whisper, the words clipped with the accent she never tried to soften despite fifteen years in London.

"No," Nell replied, equally quiet. "But Jonny suspects something. He came to the office this morning. Asked questions."

Mei's expression didn't change, but her fingers tightened almost imperceptibly on the edge of the counter. "Then we have less time than we thought."

Nell returned her nod. Without another word, Mei moved toward the back room, flipping the sign on the door to CLOSED as she passed. Nell followed, each step taken with trepidation, the floorboards creaking beneath her weight.

The back room was dimmer than she remembered, lit by a single oil lamp hanging above the table. The flame flickered as they entered, shadows that seemed to mirror Nell's unease.

Everything was ready, laid out with Mei's characteristic precision.

A flat packet wrapped in oilcloth contained the forged documents: Sally Drake's identification card, birth certificate, work reference from a factory in Manchester, and train papers. A plain traveling cloak of unremarkable brown wool rested on a hook by the door. Beside it, a carpet bag—small enough to carry without strain, large enough to hold the necessities of a new life.

Nell stood still, absorbing it all.

This was no longer theory. No longer whispered planning in the safety of darkness. It was happening.

Mei moved around the table with quiet efficiency, adjusting the hem of the coat on the hook, her movements calm and mechanical. She didn't speak again, but Nell could feel the weight of unasked questions hanging between them.

Nell let the satchel slip from her shoulder and placed it gently on the chair in the corner. For a brief second, she thought of the pocket watch inside. Of her father's voice in his final letter. Of Elijah's hand pressed to her cheek.

She closed her eyes, just for a moment.

When she opened them, Mei was watching her, something unreadable in her expression—not quite pity, not quite understanding. Something deeper.

The plan was in motion now.

There was no turning back.

CHAPTER 18

It began with a flicker small and insignificant. A single tongue of flame licking through a crack in the warehouse door. But by the time the watchman on the far end of the quay saw the first orange flare, the fire had already taken hold.

"Fire!" came the shout. "Fire at Warrington & Co!"

Men emerged from card games and loading bays, faces twisted in confusion, then horror as they saw the plume of smoke rising high above the rooftops.

The dock exploded into motion. Men ran over cobbles slick with river mist, hauling buckets from the Thames, hurling them uselessly at the growing inferno. They formed a desperate chain from the

Thames to the warehouse, hauling buckets of water and hurling them uselessly at the growing inferno. Each bucket hissed into steam upon contact, a dying breath against the monster that fed and grew with every second. Sparks spat into the night, carried aloft by the stiff breeze that howled in from the river.

In the hellish glow of the rising flames, the carved wooden sign above the entrance began to surrender. The elegant letters of *Warrington & Co.* first blackened, then peeled, and finally split with audible cracks like bones breaking.

Inside, the fire moved quickly, guided with precision through the centre of the building, fed by dry crates and oil-soaked wood, by old ledgers and packing straw. The burn was methodical in its destruction. Too perfect for an accident.

The office where Nell had sat that morning was already consumed, her desk now a pyre, the cabinet where she'd hidden her secrets belching black smoke through its drawers.

A group of workers clustered near the water's edge, buckets forgotten, staring helplessly as their livelihoods vanished in flame and ash.

"Someone run for Miss Warrington!" one cried. "She needs to know!"

Tomlinson shook his head, cap clutched in trembling hands. "I already sent for her! She's not at the house. Maid says she left early morning and hasn't come back!"

A terrible silence fell over them, broken only by the crackling roar of the fire and the distant, frantic shouts of men still trying to contain it.

"You don't think—" Frank couldn't finish the thought.

More shouting erupted from the crowd gathering at the perimeter. The clatter of hooves announced the arrival of more constables. A whistle blew sharp and fast through the chaos, ordering people back, away from danger.

And then he came, pelting through the crowds.

"Where the hell is she?!"

Jonny.

He charged through the smoke like a man possessed, shoving past the dockhands, eyes wild.

"Nell!" he bellowed. "Nell!"

The crowd turned as one.

"She's not here, Jonny," someone said. "She's not inside!"

But Jonny wasn't listening. His gaze was fixed on the burning warehouse, on the windows belching black smoke, on the doorway now framed in leaping flames.

He made for the entrance, only to be caught hard by two officers, their arms locked around his shoulders as he struggled against them.

"Let me go!" he snarled, spittle flying. "She's in there, I have to get her! She has to be in there!"

"She's not," one of the constables grunted, tightening his grip. "You'll kill yourself for nothing. Stand down, man!"

Jonny bucked violently, throwing one officer off balance. "She was working today! You don't know her like I do, she always stays late. If she's not at home, this is where she'll be!"

His voice broke on the last word, a crack that revealed something raw and desperate beneath the fury.

The flames roared louder, licking the sky now, leaping from rafter to rafter as the roof groaned and collapsed inward with a deafening crash. Sparks flew like fireworks. Smoke engulfed them all.

Jonny stopped fighting.

He sank to his knees on the wet cobbles, the fire reflected in his eyes, breathing hard.

The others backed away, as if the grief burning off him might catch.

And still the fire climbed higher, painting the river in gold and smoke, while the Warrington name turned to ash.

By the time the first light of dawn spread over the docks, the fire had gutted everything.

Where once Warrington & Co. had stood, proud and solid, there now remained only a smouldering skeleton of scorched timbers and collapsed beams. The air was thick with the soot and the stench of burnt rope, the ground still hissed with the occasional flare of dying embers.

Elijah stood at the edge of the ruin, boots sinking slightly into damp soot, his hands clenched at his sides.

The constable beside him was speaking, something about the fire watch, about arson, about inconsistencies, but Elijah barely heard. His gaze was fixed on the blackened frame of the building. On the smoke curling upward in lazy coils.

He'd known before he'd arrived.

There had been something in the tone of the messenger's voice when he'd pounded on Elijah's door at three in the morning. Something strained. Something final. A reluctance to meet his eyes, as if the news was too heavy to carry alongside eye contact.

"Warrington warehouse," the boy had gasped. "Burned to the ground. They think... you should come."

He stepped forward, past the rope the watchmen had thrown up to hold back the gathering crowd. The faces blurred together, dock workers, street sellers, a few idle gentlemen from nearby warehouses. All of them staring. Murmuring.

And then a stretcher emerged.

Two men carried it with slow, solemn care, the remains wrapped in canvas scorched black at the edges. Burnt nearly beyond recognition, but still unmistakably human in shape. A scrap of fabric clung to the shoulder, deep green, once fine, the velvet that Nell had worn the last time he saw her. As the stretcher passed, something small dislodged and fell, bouncing across the ground with a delicate chime and landing at Elijah's feet.

A small pearl hairpin, blackened at the edges but still gleaming at its center.

He'd seen that hairpin before, when he'd tucked Nell's loose curl back behind her ear, the night he'd say goodbye. When he'd told her he couldn't help her anymore.

His throat closed. His jaw locked so tight he felt his teeth ache.

THE DOCKLAND ORPHAN

Someone whispered behind him, a woman's voice thick with shocked fascination: "That's her. It has to be her. Poor soul."

He didn't move. Couldn't. His eyes remained fixed on the hairpin lying in the soot at his feet, unable to bend and pick it up, as if touching it would make this nightmare real.

A ripple went through the crowd, a shifting of bodies and attention. Heads turned. Voices hushed.

Jonny Collins appeared at the edge of the gathering, pushing through the onlookers with grim determination. His face was pale beneath a layer of stubble, his eyes bloodshot and shadowed by dark circles. The knuckles of his right hand were split and raw. He stood motionless, watching as the body passed, his shoulders tense and unreadable.

Elijah turned at last, gaze locking onto Jonny's across the space between them.

For a heartbeat, nothing moved. Not the crowd, not the smoke, not the very air between them, charged now with something volatile.

Then Elijah stepped forward. One foot. Then another. Each step deliberate, each bringing him closer to the man he held responsible for everything.

Jonny didn't move. He stood with arms loosely folded across his chest, but his posture was anything but relaxed. His eyes, usually quick with some glint of mischief or charm, held only the brewings of a storm.

"You bastard," Elijah said under his breath.

Jonny raised a brow, but his voice was low and dangerous. "Not what I'd expect to her from an officer of the law"

Elijah didn't stop. He closed the gap until they stood barely a foot apart. "You did this," Elijah said, each word precise and cutting. "You dragged her into your world of lies and filth. She tried to get out, and you couldn't let her go. She's dead because of you."

Jonny flinched, almost imperceptibly. Then his mouth twisted into something that might have been a sneer, or a grimace.

"You think I wanted this?"

"I think you'd rather see her dead than free of you," Elijah said, something dangerous uncoiling inside him.

Jonny's eyes narrowed. "You know nothing about me and Nell. Nothing."

Elijah's fist shot out before he could stop himself.

The punch landed hard across Jonny's cheek with a sickening crack, snapping his head sideways. The crowd gasped and pulled back, creating a circle around them. Blood sprayed from Jonny's mouth as he staggered, caught his footing on the slick ground, and then lunged back with a roar of fury.

They collided with the force of grief made physical. Elbows, fists, fury, scrabbling and cursing as they slammed against a stack of barrels, sending them clattering across the cobblestones. Dock hands surged forward to pull them apart, and two officers quickly intervened, wrestling between the men.

"Enough!" one shouted, grappling with Jonny's collar as he strained to break free. "That's enough!"

Elijah shook free of the man holding him and stood breathing hard, chest heaving with rage, a cut above his eye streaming blood down his face. His hat had fallen in the scuffle, his usually immaculate appearance now as disheveled as his composure.

"She was worth ten of you," he spat, blood and spittle flying. "And you'll rot in hell for what you've done."

Jonny wiped blood from his split lip with the back of his hand, smearing crimson across his cheek. His eyes blazed with an intensity that bordered on madness.

"I would've done anything for her," he said, voice cracking. "Anything she asked."

"Exactly," Elijah said coldly. "And you did. You did everything. Except let her go. Except save her."

The words hung between them, sharp as broken glass.

Another officer stepped between them, pushing them apart more forcefully now as murmurs rolled through the watching crowd.

"Move along," the constable barked. "There's been enough tragedy for one morning."

The two men were dragged back into the crowd from opposite sides, eyes still locked until the last possible second.

Tucked beneath the overhang of a shuttered tea shop, Mei Ling watched the chaos unfold. The crowd clustered tighter near the ruin of the Warrington warehouse, faces drawn in confusion, grief, and curiosity.

Word was spreading quickly now, rippling through the gathered masses like an invisible current: Miss Nell Warrington had perished in the fire. No one had seen her since the night before. A body had been recovered from the smoldering remains just after dawn.

Confirmation, the crowd whispered. Tragedy, they murmured, even as they pressed closer.

Mei saw the body being carried out, wrapped in soot-stained canvas. She saw the grief etched into familiar faces. She said nothing.

Her dark cloak blended easily into the soot-streaked alley. To most, she was just another figure, one of many drawn to the spectacle. No one looked twice.In this part of London, invisibility was a skill she had mastered long ago.

She watched Jonny Collins being held back by two constables, blood trickling from his split lip, chest heaving like a man barely holding himself together.

She saw the inspector, his face grey with shock, and that rage barely leashed beneath the surface. The force of his grief told her everything Nell had refused to admit aloud.

Mei's expression didn't shift. But her hands, folded beneath her cloak, were tight.

There would be consequences. Grief left cracks in even the most disciplined minds, and through those cracks, suspicion could creep like morning frost. Questions would follow. Investigations. Scrutiny.

She waited another moment, watching the two men pulled apart by officers, Jonny still struggling while the inspector retreated into cold formality. The tension in the crowd had begun to splinter into whispers and sidelong glances. Already, rumours were spreading like the smoke that still curled from the warehouse ruins. Had it truly been an accident? Why had Miss Warrington been there after dark? Who had been the last to see her alive?

Then Mei turned and vanished down the narrow lane behind the tea shop, skirts brushing the damp bricks as she slipped between buildings and out into the maze of alleyways that led toward the apothecary.

Her steps were light, her pace quick but controlled. She moved like someone who had done this before, this vanishing act, this slipping between the cracks of a city that preferred not to acknowledge her existence.

When she reached the apothecary, she entered through the back. She shed her cloak and shook off the ash that clung to the hem, tiny grey flecks scattering across the floorboards.

Nell was seated by the hearth, her knees drawn up under the blanket, eyes fixed on the fire as though willing it to burn away the weight in her chest. Her hair was pulled back severely, making her look older than her twenty-six years. The firelight caught the hollows beneath her cheekbones, shadows that hadn't been there a month ago.

Nell didn't look up. She didn't need to.

"Well?" she asked, her voice barely above a whisper.

Mei crossed the room and crouched beside the fire, letting the warmth chase away the lingering cold from the street.

"They believed it," she said quietly. "The body. The fire. All of it."

Nell didn't move.

Mei continued, choosing her words with care. "The inspector was there. So was Jonny. Half the neighbourhood turned out."

Now Nell turned, her breath catching. "Did they see each other?"

Mei nodded once, a small, precise movement. "Elijah saw Jonny across the crowd. He went for him. Pushed through everyone like a man possessed. There was a fight. Quick, but ugly. They had to be pulled apart."

Nell's eyes stung, tears springing hot and fast. "God."

"Jonny thinks you died in that warehouse," Mei said gently. "Elijah too. I saw his face when they pulled the body out. He looked... broken."

"I never wanted that," Nell whispered, her voice cracking. "I didn't want to hurt them. Either of them."

"You didn't want any of this," Mei said, soft but firm. "But it happened. All of it. And now we deal with the aftermath."

Nell buried her face in her hands, shoulders shaking with silent sobs. "I thought I could fix it. I thought if I got out clean, it wouldn't matter how deep I'd gone. But I ruined everything. Their lives. Mine."

Mei stood slowly and moved toward the table in the corner, where a battered leather satchel sat waiting, packed and ready. She laid a hand on it, feeling the weight of false documents, a modest sum of money, and the few possessions Nell couldn't bear to leave behind. "You need to go. Soon."

"I know," Nell said, lowering her hands to reveal reddened eyes. "I just—" Her voice cracked again. "I never got to say goodbye. Not properly."

"You said enough," Mei replied. "You left the pieces behind for them to gather however they will."

There was a long silence.

Finally, Nell wiped her face with the heel of her hand. "Do I have to go tonight?" The question carried the weight of exhaustion, physical and emotional.

"No," Mei said, folding the cloak over her arm. "You can stay here. A few more days, if needed. I'll hide you. No one comes through that back door but me."

Nell nodded, hollow. "Thank you." The words seemed inadequate for everything Mei had risked.

"But then you go," Mei added firmly. "Disappear completely. There's no other choice now. The woman they knew as Nell Warrington died in that fire."

Nell nodded again, more slowly this time, resignation settling over her.

But inside, something pulled tight in her chest. A tether still holding fast, even as the world insisted she cut the last of the cords. A persistent hope that perhaps, somehow, this wasn't truly the end of her story.

CHAPTER 19

The river had never looked so still.

Grey as slate, it lapped gently at the stone embankment near Limehouse, muffled by thick morning fog. The city beyond was little more than a blur, rooftops smudged into sky, ships' masts half-sketched in charcoal lines against the colourless dawn. Even the gulls were quiet, as if they, too, had paused to mourn.

In the distance, a small crowd had gathered outside the church. A coffin rested on trestles before them. It was plain pine, sealed tight, with thin brass handles that glinted dully in what little light filtered through the haze. A single bunch of lilies lay across it. Their white petals were already bruised at the edges, browning in the cold.

The priest, an older man with a round, wind-blown face, stood beside the coffin in faded vestments. His voice was low and hoarse from the damp, barely carrying over the persistent hum of the city going about its business.

"We gather here in grief and solemn remembrance," he said. "To honour the life of Miss Nell Warrington. A young woman taken from this world far too soon. Known to many of you, admired by more. A woman of enterprise, compassion, and rare grit."

A quiet murmur passed through the crowd. Someone sniffed. Another shifted their weight from foot to foot.

"She was," the priest continued, "by all accounts, tireless. Fair. Fiercely loyal. She gave much to this community, more than most knew, and asked for little in return."

Heads nodded. A few people wiped their eyes with rough hands or sodden handkerchiefs.

"As we commit her to the Lord's keeping," he finished gently, "let us carry forward the example she set: of integrity, of courage, and of care for those often overlooked."

A brief silence followed, broken only by the distant call of a ship's horn cutting through the fog.

Then the coffin was lowered.

The ropes creaked. The earth opened. And Nell Warrington, at least in name, was laid to rest.

Jonny Collins stood at the back of the gathering, just beyond the reach of prying eyes, his boots planted in the damp soil, his coat collar turned up against the cold.

He hadn't moved once during the service.

He hadn't blinked much, either.

His hat was pulled low over his eyes, casting a shadow that suited him, hiding whatever thoughts might be betrayed there. He said nothing. Just stood there like a statue, watching.

He watched as the dockhands removed their caps and wiped their noses. Watched as old women muttered prayers, and men shifted with the discomfort of grief that had nowhere to go. He watched every single person pass by the coffin and toss a handful of earth or a flower or a whispered goodbye.

And still, his eyes moved.

Searching.

Not for Nell.

Not anymore.

For something else.

Someone else.

The muscle in his jaw ticked as the coffin disappeared into the earth, the sound of soil pattering on the wood like soft rainfall.

Then the people began to disperse. Slowly. Quietly.

But Jonny didn't move.

He stayed where he was, gaze sharp beneath the brim of his hat, narrowing with each passing minute.

As if something didn't sit right.

A flicker of something—disappointment? relief? —passed across his face before it hardened once more into unreadable stillness.

Tucked between a stack of old crates in the alley opposite, Nell stood completely still, a ghost at her own funeral.

The cold bit at her fingers through her gloves, but she barely felt it.

She had stood there from the moment the first mourners had arrived, hidden in the half-light, her hood drawn low and her breath fogging softly in the air. Her heart pounded with each face she recognised, each voice that drifted on the breeze carrying memories she would have to learn to live without.

There they all were, her people. Her world. Standing just feet away, mourning her like she was already a memory.

She saw them cry.

She saw them nod through the priest's speech, lips pressed tight, eyes lowered in reverence for a woman who wasn't truly gone.

She watched the coffin drop and knew it wasn't her inside, but something had died all the same. A version of her, one built from duty, from survival, from sacrifice, was now sealed beneath that lid. That name, *Miss Warrington*, was no longer hers.

Her eyes scanned the crowd again.

And again.

Where was he?

She searched until her neck ached, her breath catching every time someone turned, hoping it might be him. But Elijah never came. The one face she needed most remained absent.

A cold ache settled in her chest, spreading outward until her whole body felt hollowed.

I pushed him too far.

He can't forgive me.

He's ashamed.

She swallowed hard, blinking against the sting behind her eyes that threatened to betray her even in solitude.

Maybe he never loved me as much as I hoped.

She turned away then, before the last mourner had left, unable to bear the weight of one more goodbye not meant for her ears. The silence pressing against her from the inside was louder than anything.

And for the first time, Nell truly felt like a ghost. Not because the world thought her dead, but because the one person who made her feel alive hadn't come to mourn her passing.

Nell stepped back from the edge of the alley, her cloak trailing across the slick cobbles. The last of the mourners had gone, their footsteps swallowed by the fog and the winding streets beyond.

It was done.

Her own funeral.

And still, she felt rooted to the spot, every inch of her heavy with exhaustion. The grief, the guilt, the finality, it hung over her like the river mist.

She turned, pulling the cloak tighter around her, ready to vanish back into the city's underbelly. She would return to Mei, she decided. She knew now with all certainty that there was little hope in staying, not now she knew he couldn't even bear to pay his last respects. The ache of his absence felt sharper than any blade. Tonight, she would tell Mei what she had been reluctant to admit for days:

"I'm ready to go."

She hurried forward, keen to not be seen, her

footsteps quick but measured on the wet cobblestones. The city seemed to hold its breath around her. Then a shape she hadn't noticed previously stepped from between two carriages. A man, coat dark as midnight, hat pulled low over his face like a mask.

Nell stopped dead, her blood turning to ice.

He didn't speak at first. Just moved closer, slow, deliberate.

Then:

"Are you looking for me?"

The voice was quiet, unhurried. Familiar.

Her breath caught in her throat. Her heart flipped once, painfully, against her ribs.

"Elijah?" she whispered, the name barely audible, as if speaking it too loudly might make him disappear.

He reached up and tipped his hat back, revealing eyes she had not seen since the night she watched him walk away—eyes that still saw through her, even now.

Panic surged through her. He was here to arrest her. All this time, he had been building a case. Why hadn't she left when Mei told her? Why had she lingered, foolish with hope and memory?

"I didn't mean—" she began, words tumbling over

each other like a landslide. "I know I should have told you. I didn't want to lie, not really, and I never meant for it to go so far—"

He stepped forward and pressed a finger gently to her lips, stopping the flood of desperate explanations. His touch was warm against her cold skin, and it silenced her more effectively than any shout could have.

"You shouldn't be out here," he murmured. "Let's get you back to the apothecary."

Nell stared at him, stunned into silence, searching his face for anger, for betrayal, for the disgust she had feared would come when he learned the truth. But his eyes held only concern, and something else she couldn't name.

The street was still, the fog around them curling like ribbon. Somewhere distant, a bell tolled the hour, the sound muffled and dreamy.

Nell's whole body shook, not entirely from the cold. "How do you know...?" she asked, not yet turning to face him fully, as if maintaining that small distance might protect her heart if his answer was not what she hoped. "About Mei. About the apothecary?"

"Because I'm the one who helped arrange it."

She turned slowly, disbelief warring with a sudden, dangerous hope.

"What?"

"I'm Mei's 'friend,'" he said gently, his eyes never leaving hers. "The one who got your papers. Who arranged the travel permits. Who made sure you had enough coin to start again."

Her eyes filled instantly, vision blurring with tears that felt hot against her cold cheeks.

"Why?" she whispered. "Why would you help me? After everything I did? And why didn't you tell me?"

He reached up and brushed his fingers along her cheek, catching the tear before it fell.

"Because I knew," he said quietly, "you'd never leave if you thought I still loved you. You'd stay, trying to make amends, putting yourself in danger. And I couldn't bear that."

Nell's lip trembled, hardly daring to ask the question that might shatter what little remained of her heart. "And do you? Now? Still?" Each word cost her, each syllable a step into the unknown.

He paused, but didn't look away from her.

"I do," he said finally, with such simple honesty that it broke something inside her. "God help me, Nell. I never stopped."

She stepped into him without thinking, burying

her face in his coat as the fog swirled around them. His arms came around her, strong and sure, holding her tightly as if afraid she might disappear again.

And at last, cradled against his heartbeat, she felt safe. Not the false safety of hiding, of running, of lies built upon lies, but the true safety of being known, completely, and loved anyway.

"Come," he whispered against her hair. "We don't have much time."

CHAPTER 20

The mist clung low over the Limehouse basin, a living shroud curling around ropes and pilings and swallowing the sound of footsteps before they landed. It was the kind of fog that blurred outlines, and gave London the strange illusion of softness.

Nell stood at the edge of the dock with her hood drawn low and her hands clutched around the worn leather satchel tucked beneath her cloak. The weight of it pressed against her ribs. Inside were papers with a name that didn't belong to her. Not yet. Soon, though, it would be the only name she answered to.

The barge bobbed gently against the mooring, squat and unimpressive, laden with sacks of grain and tarpaulin-covered crates that glistened with dew. Water lapped against its weathered hull. Exactly the kind of vessel no one would bother to inspect too closely. No one remembered the ordinary. It was perfect.

Behind her, Elijah stepped quietly into place, his coat brushing hers as he paused beside her. He didn't speak. Neither of them had said much since leaving the apothecary. The words had all been spent the night before. Promises made, confessions whispered, forgiveness granted in the quiet hours when the world seemed far away.

At the far end of the dock, just beyond the reach of the lanternlight, Mei stood watching. Her dark hair was pinned in its usual practical knot, her hands folded before her with quiet precision. Beside her, one of the apothecary boys waited with a paper parcel, his eyes fixed on the planks beneath his feet. He wouldn't meet Nell's eyes, too young to understand that sometimes salvation required deception.

Nell crossed the dock in silence. When she reached her, Mei handed her the parcel. Inside, Nell knew were the last things she'd take from London. Coin, papers, and a handful of dried herbs that would help with sleep.

"You'll never outrun the past," Mei said, her voice

low, steady. "But you can choose who walks with you from here on."

Nell's throat tightened. "I never could've done this without you."

"It's nothing." Mei's eyes softened, just a fraction, the only crack in her careful composure. "Now go, before you change your mind. Before someone sees what shouldn't be seen."

They didn't embrace. They never had. Such gestures weren't their language. But Mei touched her arm briefly, fingers pressing into the fabric of her cloak, and it said everything of the friendship had built between them.

Nell nodded, then turned back.

She and Elijah climbed aboard. The deck shifted slightly beneath their boots. The deckhand, a boy no older than seventeen, one of Mei's team, cast off the rope without a word and poled them out into the current with efficiency.

The city faded almost immediately, as if London itself was complicit in their escape. As the barge turned downstream, the banks disappeared behind a wall of grey, and the dock became a shadow.

Nell stayed at the stern, eyes fixed on the place where the mooring had been.

Only when it was gone did she breathe.

The river moved beneath them, slow and silent. The barge cut a gentle path through the fog, its wake vanishing before it ever reached the banks. The sky overhead was beginning to pale, shifting from soot-grey to the barest hint of silver.

Nell stood at the stern, the cold biting at her cheeks, turning them to rose against her pale skin. The wind lifted strands of her hair from beneath her hood, tugging them free, copper threads catching what little light filtered through the mist.

London was gone. Somewhere behind them, the dock where she had once commanded men and managed cargo was now just another memory. A place she'd burned to the ground with her name inside it.

She let out a long, trembling breath and watched it dissolve into the air.

Elijah stepped beside her. He didn't speak. He didn't need to.

They stood like that for a long time, side by side, the quiet between them weightless but full.

Finally, Nell said, "I still can't believe you did it."

He looked at her. "Did what?"

"You gave it all up. Your job. Your standing. Everything."

His expression didn't waver. "I gave up a uniform

I hated. A city that eats its own. And a system that would've seen you hang for a crime committed out of loyalty."

He reached for her hand, his fingers finding hers with the certainty of someone who had memorised the map of her skin. She let him take it, her cold fingers warming in his grasp.

"I didn't give up everything," he said softly, the words meant only for her. "I chose something better."

Her eyes filled with sudden heat, the tears sharp and unexpected. "You'll never be able to go back. They'll brand you a traitor, a criminal, worse than me."

"I don't want to," he said simply, as if it were the easiest choice in the world. Perhaps for him, it had been.

She leaned her head against his shoulder, the wool of his coat rough against her cheek, and together they watched the river carry them further from the city, further from everything they'd lost, closer to what they might find.

"What now?" she asked, her voice thin in the wind.

He glanced toward the open river. "We disappear now."

She shook her head, a small smile tugging at the corner of her mouth. "No. We begin."

He looked at her properly then, his expression softening. "We begin," he echoed.

"A new life," she said, the words gathering strength as she spoke them. "Where we can forget the past. Where no one knows our names or our sins. Where we can live unburdened at last."

He reached into his coat pocket and pulled something out. A small, warped piece of brass, blackened at the edges. It was twisted, half-melted by flames that had claimed a warehouse and a life that no longer existed, but still legible.

WARRINGTON & CO.

She stared at it, this artifact from a life that no longer belonged to her.

"I found it in the ash," he said quietly. "I couldn't let them erase you completely. Some things deserve to be remembered, even if only by us."

NELL TOOK IT FROM HIM, turning it over in her hand. The engraving was almost gone.

She stepped to the side of the boat, held the brass plate above the water for one long breath, a silent farewell to the woman she had been, to the life that was now behind her, and then let it fall.

It sank without a sound, disappearing into the murky depths where doubtless other secrets rested.

She didn't look back. There was nothing there for her now.

As the barge glided on, she reached for Elijah's hand. He took it, no hesitation, his fingers interlacing with hers.

And together they stood, quiet and still, as the last remnants of their old life sunk to the bottom of the Thames, and the horizon began to open up before them.

The sun was rising, weak and pale behind the lingering mist. A faint golden hue settled over the rooftops, turning the chimney smoke into ribbons of light and shadow.

On a narrow iron bridge above the Thames, Jonny Collins stood alone.

He leaned against the railing, his gloved hands resting casually on the iron, but there was nothing casual in his expression. His eyes were sharp beneath the brim of his hat, tracking the slow movement of the barge cutting across the water below.

No mistaking it.

There she was. Hood low, but he recognised those unruly strands of copper hair escaping from beneath it. Those straight proud shoulders, standing at the prow with her hand in his. That bloody inspector. The one who always acted too clean for the likes of them.

So that was how it had ended. Not with a body in the ground, but with a trick. A disappearing act worthy of a penny theatre, with London itself as the stage.

His jaw tightened, muscle working beneath the skin. The cigarette between his fingers burned to the nub, orange against the grey morning. He flicked it into the water, watching it hiss and die.

"Thought you were clever, didn't you?" he muttered, his words carried away by the wind. "A funeral, a fire, a new name. As if that's all it takes to become someone else."

The barge passed directly beneath him, close enough that if he shouted, they might hear. Close enough that if he had a pistol, they'd never see another sunrise.

He didn't move. Just watched.

Watched as it slipped downriver and disappeared into the fog, two figures standing side by side like carved figurines on a ship's prow, like the past hadn't already begun catching up with them, like the world would let them escape so easily.

"You won't get away from me that easily, Warrington," he murmured, rolling her name on his tongue like a promise. "No one does."

He turned slowly, the fog swirling around his coat like ghostly fingers as he disappeared into it, leaving nothing but the echo of his promise behind and the certainty that some stories never truly end.

Only pause, before the next chapter begins.

THE END

STAY IN TOUCH

Be the first to hear about my brand new books.

Sign up to my list and get a FREE book "A Mother's Hope" delivered straight to your Kindle, Tablet or EReader.

CLICK BELOW

https://dl.bookfunnel.com/vr7mq3vnjt

ALSO BY LILY BOURNE

The Bennet Sisters Trilogy

The Daughter's Burden

The Daughter's Revenge

The Daughter's Justice

CLICK HERE TO FIND OUT MORE

Printed in Great Britain
by Amazon